Ask Amy Green

BRIDESMAID BLITZ

Ask Amy Green

BRIDESMAID BLITZ

SARAH WEBB

CANDLEWICK PRESS

First U.S. edition 2012

Library of Congress Cataloging-in-Publication Data
Webb, Sarah.
Ask Amy Green : bridesmaid blitz / Sarah Webb. — 1st U.S. ed.
p. cm.
Summary: To prepare for her mother's wedding, thirteen-year-old Amy and her seventeen-year-old Aunt Clover go from Dublin, Ireland, to Paris to shop for the perfect bridesmaid dress.
ISBN 978-0-7636-5157-2
[1. Shopping—Fiction. 2. Dresses—Fiction. 3. Bridesmaids—Fiction. 4. Aunts—Fiction. 5. Paris (France)—Fiction. 6. France—Fiction.]
I. Title. II. Title: Bridesmaid blitz.
PZ7.W3838Asd 2012
[Fic]—dc23 2011018623

12 13 14 15 16 17 RRC 10 9 8 7 6 5 4 3 2 1

Printed in Crawfordsville, IN, U.S.A.

This book was typeset in Giovanni.

Candlewick Press
99 Dover Street
Somerville, Massachusetts 02144

visit us at www.candlewick.com

Hi there, or should I say, *Salut*.

Welcome to *Bridesmaid Blitz*. You are about to share Amy and Clover's adventures in one of the most magical cities in the world: Paris.

I worked at a McDonald's in Paris while I was a student, cooking fries and garnishing hamburgers (exciting stuff!), and while I was there I grew to love the city, with its dramatic buildings, amazing art galleries, and *boulangeries*, or French bakeries, and their delicious yeasty bread.

Last year I went back — special birthday treat — and stayed in a beautiful little hotel in Montmartre. Like Amy, I visited the Pompidou Centre, braved the crowds to pay homage to the *Mona Lisa* in the Louvre, and sat outside cafés, people watching, which is one of my favorite things to do in the whole world. And I fell passionately in love with the city all over again.

If you ever get a chance to visit Paris, go, go, go! I know you'll just adore it. And for pics of my birthday trip and some of my very favorite things to do and see in the city, check out my website: **www.askamygreen.com**.

♥ *À bientôt,* *
Sarah XXX ♥

* "Later, alligator" in French!

♥ Chapter 1

"I'm *soooo* depressed," I moan. "I can't believe we're back at school tomorrow. Kill me now." I grab my best friend Mills's hair straightener and pretend to stab myself in the heart. "O happy dagger . . . let me die." Then I stagger backward, fall onto her bed, and squash her against the star-patterned duvet.

"Ow, Amy! Get off me, you eejit," she squeals. "And stop with all the Shakespeare. I don't want to be reminded of English class, thanks very much."

I laugh and roll sideways. We both lie on our backs, staring up at the ceiling. There's something stuck to it. A photo. I squint up my eyes, then grin. Ed Whooley's tanned face is smiling down at us.

"Nice pic," I say.

Ed is Mills's cute-as-Christmas boyfriend. But there's one rather ginormous relationship glitch: he lives in America. They hooked up over the summer hols while Mills was working as an au pair in his hometown of Miami, and they've been exchanging smoochy e-mails ever since.

Ed also happens to be Matt Munroe's little bro — yep, *that* Matt Munroe, the actor who makes R-Patz look ugly. My crazy aunt Clover had to interview Matt in Miami for the teen mag she works for — the *Goss* — and guess who got to travel to the U.S. of A-mazing with her? You got it, li'l ol' *moi*.

It turned out Matt Munroe was only pretending to be American and is actually 100-percent-guaranteed Irish beef, and Clover scooped the story for the *Goss*. It was quite the trip!

Mills goes pink at the mention of the photo. "You weren't supposed to see that."

I chuckle. "And how is Ed the Head?"

"Fine." Long pause. "I think. I haven't heard from him all week. I've sent eight e-mails now. I tried ringing his cell but he didn't answer, and I rang his house twice but his dad said he wasn't there. He hasn't rung back yet, and Mum's going to kill me when she sees the phone bill. Maybe he hasn't been getting his messages and there's something wrong with Hotmail. Should I send another e-mail?"

I wince. "Not unless you want him to think you're a serious stalker. Sorry, Mills, it doesn't sound good."

"Maybe he's just really busy?" she suggests hopefully.

Poor Mills. Ed is her first proper boyfriend. I have to tread softly. "Maybe. Methinks you should leave it a few days, though — see if he gets back to you."

She sighs deeply. "Relationships are tough."

"I hear you, *amigo*. Seth's been acting odd recently too."

"At least you both live in the same time zone. Plus, you'll get to see him in school tomorrow."

I groan. "Don't remind me."

Mills's eyes open wide. "I thought it was true *lurrvve*. Have you gone off him?"

"'Course not. Seth and I are grand," I say, then add in a stage Irish accent, "Sure, he's the joy of me heart, me *acushla*." I conjure up an image of my boyfriend's face in my head — warm smile, messy blond surfer hair, sun freckles sprinkled over the bridge of his nose, and startling sky-blue eyes. "I was groaning about school. Speaking of which, when's the school trip to Paris?"

"In two weeks. I can't wait," she shrieks, then hugs herself with excitement. But she stops when she sees my fed-up face. "Sorry, Ames. I wish you could come too. It won't be the same without you. And Seth's not the only one who'll miss you like crazy." She rubs her head on my shoulder and makes sad-puppy noises.

I sigh. "If I'd known there was a trip involved I would have chosen ze froggy language with Loopy, instead of Spanish. Plus, her classes sound way more fun."

Mills laughs. "Miss Lupin does try to keep us awake, all right. The best was the Paris Fashion Week role-playing. We all had to pretend to be models, or designers, or fashion journalists and act in character. I was Anna Wintour from *Vogue*. It was hilarious."

She pauses and her expression shifts. "Until Annabelle and Sophie had a catfight over who was going to be Kate Moss. Sophie swung her bag at Annabelle and nearly took one of her front teeth out."

I laugh. "I remember that. Mrs. Hamilton threatened to sue Loopy for endangering her daughter's perfect smile."

Annabelle Hamilton is Queen Bee of the D4s — the school's resident mean girls. They're named after the postcode of one of the poshest areas in Dublin:

Dublin 4. None them actually live there, except for Annabelle herself—her girls-in-waiting, Sophie Piggott and Nina Pickering, live in Foxrock and Cabinteely—but that doesn't stop them from acting like they're better and heaps cooler than everyone else.

Mills makes a face. "I'm not looking forward to seeing Annabelle and her cronies again. I bet the D4s all have sparkling new uniforms. And I'll be stuck in last year's gear and the same scuffed ballet pumps I've been wearing all summer. I'm in for a right D4 slag-a-rama. I know they're going to call me Little Orphan Annie again. And Annabelle's bound to have this season's designer shoes."

"Bound to," I say. "But there's always sabotage. I'll help you pull the soles off your shoes or something, then you'll have to get a new pair."

Mills sighs. "Wouldn't work. Mum would just get them fixed. You know she's an eco-fiend and probably the only person in the universe who still darns socks. No, I'll just have to put up with it."

"If it's any consolation, I'll be in my old Dubes. We'll be the Sorry Shoe Twins. *Très* depressing."

We both sigh and stare up at Ed again.

"Ames, what am I going to do?" Mills says softly. "About Ed, I mean."

"I'll ask Clover." Clover's seventeen and *über*

worldly. I figure the bad news is better coming from Clover than from me. Clover's great at solving problems. As agony aunt for the *Goss*, she's had buckets of practice. She loves answering all the readers' problem letters. And I get to help her. Lately, they've started printing my name on the page and everything. How cool is that?

Yep, if anyone can help, Clover can.

Mills smiles. "Thanks. But don't tell her it's me, OK? It's so embarrassing."

"Promise." Unfortunately, Clover's so smart she'll probably figure it out in a nanosecond.

I check my watch. "Oops, better motor. Mum threatened me with yearlong grounding if I wasn't back by eight. And I'm already late."

"Last night of freedom before we meet our *dooooom*." Mills clutches her neck and pretends to choke herself. "Guess I'll see you at the postbox. Usual time."

I wink. "It's a date, honeybun."

♥ Chapter 2

I sprint toward my house. Mills and I both live in the same estate, Sycamore Park in Glenageary. We've been friends since we were old enough to share Barbie dolls. She lives at number 21 — our place is number 15 — so every school day we meet at the green postbox in front of Mills's and travel in together on the DART. Mum can't understand why we need to spend so much time "in each other's pockets," as she puts it, but I guess that's because she's nearly forty. Her priorities are all over the place.

Dad's Mercedes is parked outside my house, and I'm so not in the humor for yet another pep talk about how "second year is the foundation for the Junior Cert. exams," so "there's to be no coasting" and "you must take it seriously"—yadda yadda yadda. I plan to creep in and dash upstairs without getting spotted, but Mum catches me in the hall.

"What time do you call this, young lady?" she asks crossly.

"Eight?"

She taps her watch face. "Twenty past. Your dad's in the kitchen waiting for you."

My little brother, Alex, appears at the top of the stairs in his Thomas the Tank Engine pajamas, his cheeks pink and shiny from the bath, his white-blond hair standing up wild and fuzzy, like a dandelion. He looks delighted with himself. Even though he's only two in October, he loves a good upside-down blow-dry.

"Get back into bed, buster," Mum hisses up the stairs.

He shrieks with laughter and scampers off.

"He'd better not wake Evie," Mum says darkly. "I swear I'm going to put bars across the top of his cot one of these days. He's a mini David Blaine." (Evie's my baby sister, and she's a divil to get back to sleep.)

Mum gives one of her theatrical sighs. "Dave's never here when I need him."

Dave lives with us. He's Mum's boyfriend. Scratch that, fiancé — he proposed recently on a beach in West Cork, and it was actually quite romantic for two olds.

"Is he at work?" I ask, then immediately wish I hadn't. Oops, I should learn to keep my mouth shut. Cue the Mamma Moan.

She rolls her eyes. "As always. He should be here, helping me with the kids. But if he's not hiding away, working on those ridiculous songs, he's in that stupid hospital, looking after strangers."

Before he had the babies with Mum, Dave used to be a singer-songwriter, and in between nursing at Saint Vincent's Hospital he's working on a range of rock nursery rhymes for toddlers featuring a fluffy yellow character called Dinoduck, who's half duck, half dinosaur. I kid you not!

Mum brushes a lank clump of hair that has escaped from her ponytail back off her face. The bags under her eyes are the color of fresh bruises. Poor Mum — she looks wrecked.

"I think that's what nurses are supposed to do — look after people," I say gently, sensing she's a tad fragile this evening. "It's their job."

She rubs her sockets with her knuckles, smearing her mascara. "Sorry, Amy. I've just had a long day. Alex is exhausting at the moment, and Clover keeps bothering me about the wedding plans."

"She's only trying to help."

"I know. But I have enough to worry about. There's

plenty of time to stress about table arrangements and wedding cakes."

"If you're still getting married on New Year's Eve, you only have four months," I point out.

She looks horrified. "Four months? Are you sure?"

"Yep. Wednesday is the first of September."

Mum puts her hands over her face and starts to moan.

I think for a second and then say, "I recorded *Grey's Anatomy* for you. Why don't you go and watch it? Would a cup of tea help?"

She peels her hands away and starts to perk up a little. "No, but dreamy doctors and a large glass of wine just might. I haven't sat down all day."

When I walk into the kitchen to get Mum her wine, Dad's on his hunkers rooting through one of the cupboards. Mum hates when he does that. She says it hasn't been his house for years and it's an invasion of her privacy. I think she's just embarrassed by the state of her cupboards. Dad's new wife, Shelly, keeps their house immaculate, not a biscuit crumb out of place. White carpets, white sofas, white walls, with touches of silvery gray — her accent color, apparently; whatever that means — it's like living in a show house.

"Make yourself at home," I say dryly.

He stands up quickly, looking a little guilty. "Oh, hi, Amy. I'm on the scrounge for chocolate. My blood sugar levels are all over the place."

There's nothing wrong with Dad's blood sugar. What he really means is: "Help, I'm a chocoholic. I need a fix." Luckily, Dave's also Mr. Sweet Tooth. It's about the only thing they have in common, apart from Mum, of course. I click my finger against the child lock, open Dave's special drawer, and hand over a Mars bar.

"Thanks." He sits down at the kitchen table and starts to dunk it in his mug of tea, making the chocolate go all slimy. Yuck.

I pour a large glass of wine from the bottle in the fridge. "Back in a second, Dad."

"That'd better be for your mother, young lady," he says, giving me a mock serious look.

"It is. I'm more of a mojito girl myself," I joke. A mojito is Clover's favorite cocktail. It's white rum with lime and mint. Even though she's not a big drinker — she likes being in control and says life's difficult enough to navigate without dulling your senses — she's a whiz at mixing cocktails and appoints herself Head Bar Girl at all Gramps's parties. Gramps is Clover's dad and my grampa, but we all call him Gramps.

Dad laughs a little uneasily. I think he still sees me as a little girl whose only knowledge of drink is Ribena and fizzy Fanta Orange.

Once Mum is settled on the sofa, clutching a glass and sighing over Meredith Grey's complicated love life, I return to the kitchen.

Dad's still dunking and munching. Boy, that man can devour a Mars bar — it's nearly all gone. Wiping traces of chocolate from the edges of his mouth, he looks up and smiles at me. "Have a present for you." He picks a Champion Sports bag off the floor and hands it to me. "Wanted to get you something. New year at school and all that. Hope they're the right size."

I pull out a pair of navy yoga pants and give a little squeal. They're heaps better than my gross pleated gym skirt that looks like an old-fashioned lamp shade. When I asked Mum for a pair, she handed me a tenner and told me to get some tracky bottoms at Penneys. I just sighed and handed it straight back, only to be given the usual "money doesn't grow on trees" lecture.

I hold them up against me and smile. "Thanks, Dad."

"Sylvie said you were after a pair." He chomps on the final nub of the Mars bar, then swallows before saying, "All set for school?"

I bundle the yoga pants into the bag and hang it on the back of the chair. "Kind of. But let's not talk about that — too depressing. How's Bump?" (Shelly's pregnant and I've just about gotten my head around having another sproglet sibling.)

"Kicking away. Shelly's finding it hard to sleep. Makes her a bit grouchy. Roll on October."

I'm about to say, "Duh, she's Oscar the Grouch anyway, Dad," but I bite my tongue. I'm trying to be nicer to Dad's new wife these days on account of the baby. "Would you like a boy or girl?" I say instead.

"Shelly's dying for a girl — says the clothes are nicer — but I don't really mind either way." Dad turns the Mars bar wrapper inside out and starts to lick it.

"Dad, please. That's disgusting."

He puts the wrapper down. "Sorry."

"Any idea of names for the baby?" I ask.

"Yes. But it keeps changing. Last week, Shelly liked Amber or Wallis for a girl, and Oliver for a boy. This week, it's Willow and Jonah. Or Justin."

"Dad! Justin's the dog's name. You can't name the baby after your dog. Anyway, what are *your* choices? It's your baby too."

"Alice, maybe? Martha? Rosie? I like old-fashioned names. And for a boy: Jack."

"Jack." I nod, smiling. "Much better than Justin."

Mum walks in the door then, wineglass in hand. She puts it down on the kitchen table. It's still half full. "What's better than Justin, Amy? What are you talking about?" She sounds slightly worried.

"We're discussing baby names, Mum, OK?"

She looks relieved. "Jack Green," she says slowly, testing it out. "I like it. What about your girls' names, Art?"

"Shelly likes Willow." I throw my eyes to heaven as I say it.

A smile flickers over Mum's lips. "Willow Green? Sorry, Art, but it sounds like a color on a paint chart."

"How about Arminta Green?" I suggest. "Minty Green is cute."

Mum claps her hands together. "I've got it. Pepper Minty Green."

"That's not very helpful, girls," Dad says. But I can tell he's trying not to laugh.

"Anyway, the name has to fit the baby," I say. "Evie was going to be Alice, but it didn't suit her, did it, Mum?"

Mum nods. "She had loads of dark hair and her face was all squished up, like a little pixie. She wasn't an Alice."

"So I think you should wait until you see the baby before deciding," I tell him.

Dad smiles. "You're quite right, Amy. I'll pass your words of wisdom on to Shelly. Let's hope she'll go for it; otherwise, I think your half-brother or sister may have a tough time in school."

Half-brother or sister? That's a funny thing to say. I know it's technically correct, but Alex and Evie are half-siblings too and they sure feel like the real deal to me. Maybe Dad thinks this baby won't be as important to me on account of Shelly and everything, or because I won't be living with them every day, but he's wrong, so wrong!

I stare at him, but he doesn't seem to notice.

Mum's oblivious too. She yawns so deeply her jaw cracks. "Ouch," she says, rubbing it. "Right, I'm off to bed."

I laugh. "It's not even nine yet, Mum."

"I know. Pathetic, isn't it? One sip of the wine and my eyes started to droop." She sloshes the rest down the sink — the fruity smell wafts around the kitchen for a second — and then yawns again. "Bit of a waste, but can't be helped. Bed by nine thirty, young lady, and don't forget to organize your bag. You have school in the morning."

I groan. "Don't remind me."

Dad stands up then and dumps his mug in the sink. "Best get going. Shelly doesn't like being alone at the moment. I keep telling her she's not going to pop for at least another month, but she's convinced she'll go early like her mum. I'll see you this weekend, Amy. I have a golf tournament in Wexford, followed by a dinner, but I'll be back first thing Sunday morning. OK?"

"But what about Saturday night?" I say.

"Shelly will order in pizza. And you can watch a movie together."

"You won't be there?"

Dad sucks his teeth. "No. It's an important tournament. I really need to play."

I start to panic. Shelly and I don't exactly get on. "Why don't I come over the following weekend instead?"

"It'll be fine. You and Shelly can have a girls' night. It'll be fun." Dad goes to rub my hair, but I jerk my head away.

Fun, I think. Are you deranged? Shelly's crazy and she hates me. And the feeling's mutual. I want to tell him this but don't like upsetting him — I get to see him little enough as it is. So although I feel like yelling at him, I say nothing.

I can tell Mum's not impressed, though. She's staring at him, her eyes like fireworks. "Art, can't you see that Amy's not exactly thrilled about being dumped with Shelly for the whole weekend?" she says.

Dad runs his hands through his hair. "It's hardly the whole weekend. Just one night. And it's not really any of your business, Sylvie."

Mum gives a high-pitched squeak then opens her mouth to say something, but I step in quickly. I HATE when they argue. "How about I come over on Sunday instead, Dad? We could go for pizza then, just the two of us. Shelly could stay home and rest." I look at him hopefully.

He's gnawing on his lip. "This golf tournament is a big deal, Amy. Padraig Harrington's playing. And because Shelly hates being on her own at the moment, I can't go to Wexford unless—"

Mum gasps. "Now I get it. You want Amy to stay over to keep Shelly company for you. Art, that's appalling!"

Dad looks sheepish. "You're not really helping, Sylvie."

"Helping?" Mum gives a rather manic laugh. "Like I care. You're the most selfish man on the planet, Art Green. Just listen to yourself—trying to use Amy as some sort of babysitter for Shelly because she's too fluffy to cope on her own for one night." She turns to me. "Tell your father you'll see him the weekend after next, Amy. You'll be spending this weekend at home."

Dad's face drops. "What about my golf tournament?"

"Frankly, you can shove your golf tournament where the sun don't shine. Now, Amy needs her sleep. Good-bye." Mum holds open the kitchen door.

Dad looks at me, unleashing his hound-dog eyes. "Amy, I just need you to do this one thing for me. And when I'm back on Sunday, we'll do pizza, I promise. Just the two of us. Please? I don't ask for much."

I stare back at him. What? Is he serious? Spending a whole evening with Shelly would be a *humongous* ask at any time, but she's even more neurotic now she's preggers. Only . . . he looks so sad now, and suddenly I don't know what to do. Dad is golf mad — it's his obsession. And he has some sort of weird man-crush on Padraig Harrington, the Irish God of Golf; he even has this special signed photograph of him. And I do want to make Dad happy.

I shrug. "OK, I'll do it."

"Amy, you don't have to —" Mum says, but I interrupt her.

"On three conditions," I continue. "One: it had better be a stonkingly good pizza. Two: I'm not watching any of those horror films Shelly likes. And three: I charge ten euro an hour for babysitting. So that will be what, about two hundred euro."

Dad chortles. "Good one, Amy."

But I'm not smiling and the grin drops off his face pretty quickly.

"Shelly's not a child," he says.

I raise an eyebrow and Mum snorts.

"I think you're getting off lightly, Art," she says.

"I've just given Amy expensive yoga pants," Dad protests. "And ten euro an hour is extortionate."

"And now I'm saving up for new runners," I say. "To go with the yoga pants."

Dad runs his hands through his hair. "You drive a hard bargain, Amy, but OK — you babysit Shelly on Saturday night and I'll give you fifty euro for runners."

I give a laugh. "Bought runners recently, Dad?"

"OK, seventy. That's my final offer. Deal?" He sticks out his hand for me to shake.

"You two are as bad as each other." Mum shakes her head, and off she huffs.

I clasp his hand. His palm feels warm and smooth. I'd prefer a hug, to be honest — shaking hands with your own dad seems a bit odd — and I'm still not thrilled that he's chosen golf over spending time with me, but I'm used to it at this stage. And

I didn't really expect him to pay me for keeping an eye on Shelly—I was only joking—so I guess it's an added bonus.

I see Dad out and then creep into the living room to watch some telly. I know Mum asked me to sort out my textbooks for school a week ago and I still haven't done it, but there's no way, José, I'm going to waste my last few precious hours of holiday time on that. Besides, I need some de-stressing after having to witness Mum and Dad bickering again. I find *Glee* on the Sky box and settle down to watch Rachel belt out yet another show tune.

Ten minutes later, there's a loud *BANG* as something slaps the window, hard, and I nearly jump out of my skin.

Peeling back the curtains, I peer out into the murky night and suddenly a face appears at the window. It's pressed up against the glass like something out of one of Shelly's horror films. I give a breathy shriek.

♥ Chapter 3

As the face draws back, I realize it's not a vampire or a burglar; it's Clover. I hurry into the hall and open the front door.

"Yowser, Beanie. How goes it?" she says, a big stupid grin on her face.

"*Pógarooney*, Clover. Are you trying to kill me?" I ask, my heart still almost thumping out of my chest.

She just chuckles and shakes her head. "You're so easy to scare; I couldn't resist. Are you going to let me in?"

"I guess," I say a little crossly, standing back from the doorway. "But I'm supposed to be in my room, so shush, OK?"

Clover makes a scene of tiptoeing into the living room, bending her body over and putting her finger to her lips, like she's on the stage. I follow and close the door carefully behind us. She flops onto the sofa, swivels around, dangles her feet over the armrest, and folds her arms behind her head.

"Quite comfortable?" I ask her.

"Yes, thanks," she replies, ignoring my snarky tone. "What has you in such a grump?"

"What were you doing out there, anyway?" I say, ignoring her question. I perch on the side of the armchair and glare down at her.

"Practicing my superstealth technique. You never know when you might need to spy on someone. I was out there for ages before you spotted me."

"Spotted you? Clover, your face was gurning against the window. I could hardly miss you."

She shrugs. "I got bored of the surveillance. You weren't even picking your nose or scratching your bum."

"Clover!"

"What? Everyone picks their nose when they think no one's looking, Beanie. Don't be such a girlie wuss. Anyway, what were you watching? At one stage, you seemed to be singing along."

"*Glee,*" I admit. "And I'd like to get back to it before Mum catches me, so get to the point."

"The point?"

"What are you doing here, Clover? It's after nine and you know Mum's a bedtime Nazi on school nights. I'm supposed to be upstairs, getting my stuff sorted out for school tomorrow."

Clover wrinkles her nose. "School-smool. Real life is far more important than stupid old lessons and exams, Bean Machine."

I sigh. "So true."

"Besides, I haven't seen a soul all day. Brains is gigging in Cork, and Gramps is in Belfast with his old RTÉ buddies at some sort of awards thingy. I've been rattling around the house all day on my ownio. I tried to do some work but gave up after staring at a blank screen for an hour." She gives me a half smile that doesn't reach her eyes and then looks away. "Just wanted some company, I guess," she adds softly.

My irritation at being spied on (and being pulled away from *Glee*) melts away. Clover rarely admits to feeling anything other than fab, so owning up to feeling lonely is a big deal.

"Things OK at the mag?" I ask gently.

She shakes her head. "Not really. Remember the intern I was telling you about — Saskia Davenport?"

"The posh one who looks like a vampire and only wears black?"

"The very minx." Clover pretends to put her

finger down her throat and gag. "She's still biting at my heels, like an evil job-stealing Alsatian. She keeps asking Saffy if she can 'help' me with the agony aunt pages. It's making me an ultraparanoid android." (Saffy is Clover's editor at the *Goss*, and she sounds pretty scary.) "My brain's nearly fried from thinking up new articles and keeping on top of the agony aunt pages. This month's postbag is Bleak House — pathetic letters asking how to cure warts and how to find the perfect pair of jeans — what do they think I am, an embarrassing-bodies-doctor-cum-stylist? There's nothing with the 'universal appeal' that Saffy's always banging on about. And I'm so out of feature-creature ideas it's unreal. Sad, sad state of affairs, Bean Machine." She looks really glum, which is so unlike Clover. She needs serious cheering up and distraction.

"I've got an idea for you," I say. "A piece on long-distance romances and how to keep them alive — you know, after the summer holidays and everything. And how to cope if things go belly-up. It's a common problem. Very 'universal.'" I smile at her brightly.

Clover cocks her head and looks me in the eye. "Is it, now?" The edges of her lips lift. "Everything hunky-D with Seth? Or is it Mills and her li'l slice of the American Dream?"

You can't keep anything from Clover. I knew she'd guess. "It's Ed. He's gone incommunicado. Hasn't contacted Mills for a whole week. And they used to IM every day. She's been e-mailing and ringing — she even talked to his dad — but still *nada*."

"*Siúcra*." Clover sucks her lips, making a faint hiss — but she seems brighter now that she has someone else's problem to focus on. "Not good. Sounds like Ed's moving on to pastures *nouveaux*. Poor Mills." She shakes her head sadly. "Not much you can do, Beanie. Just be there for her and help her find a worthy successor as quickly as possible, to help her take her mind off him. A real prince. But I do believe you've put your finger on something there." She whips her notebook out of her utterly swoony red vintage Birkin bag ("borrowed" from the *Goss* fashion cupboard) and talks slowly as she starts scribbling. "'How to Make Your Summer Lovin' Last and How to Cope When It All Goes Belly-up.'"

She reads it back to herself then looks up. "Bean Machine, you're a genius. You may have just saved my bacon. Finally, I'll have something decent to show Saffy. Oh, and I almost forgot . . ." She digs around in her bag again and pulls out a square of dark-pink tissue paper. "This is for you." She thrusts the packet into my hands. "Happy 'back to school,' Beanie. Enjoy second year — it's stellar. No major exams, and oceans of time to hang with your friends — what's not to love?"

I peel back the tissue paper and beam. It's only the Alexander McQueen scarf I spotted in the *Goss*'s last issue. It's beautiful — black, dotted with tiny dark-pink skulls with angel wings. I'm about to thank Clover when there's a noise from the hall.

"Amy? Amy? Is that you down there?"

It's Mum.

Still clutching the scarf, I leap up to open the living-room door before she comes down the stairs and finds Clover here. She's standing at the top of the stairs in her baggy striped pajamas.

"Thought I heard voices," she says. "What's going on? Why aren't you in your room, young lady?"

"Just switching off the television — you were so tired you must have left it on, Mum. Go back to bed."

"Right. OK. Well, don't be too long." She shuffles away, yawning.

After she's gone, Clover appears behind me. "Better mush," she whispers. "Don't want to get you into trouble with Sylvie. And thanks for the feature-creature. Smooch, smooch." She kisses the tips of her fingers, blows them at me, and flies out the front door, her bag slapping against her hip.

I run my fingers over the scarf and smile to myself. "Thanks, Clover. You rock."

♥ Chapter 4

"Would you look at that piece of fine in the Saint John's uniform?" Mills nods at the boy standing beside the doors of the DART, listening to his iPod. It's hard not to stare. He's tall and tanned, with emerald eyes and chiseled cheekbones that angels would fight to hang their wings on. Under his slouchy gray beanie, his hair is jet-black.

I grin at her and whistle under my breath. "Bom-chicka-wha-wha."

"Amy!" Seth isn't impressed.

"You know I only have eyes for you." I kiss the tips of my fingers and blow them at him, Clover-style.

He laughs. "Keep it that way."

"Must be his first day," Mills says. "Poor guy. I'd hate to be a newbie. Wonder if he's in our year."

Seth looks him up and down. "Nah. Too tall. I'd say third or Transition."

Annabelle Hamilton and Sophie Piggott totter past us on their spindle heels, legs, hands, and faces fake-baked the D4s' signature dark orange. I'm surprised to see them together; they had a falling-out recently — Sophie snogged Annabelle's boyfriend, Mark Delaney, at the end-of-term party, in her garden shed, no less. They've obviously made up now, though. It's hard to keep up with D4 politics, so generally I don't bother.

Sophie used to be our friend up until the summer when she was consumed into the bowels of the D4 posse. I think Mills misses her sometimes, but I most certainly don't. She's catty, bitter, and as twisted as a *Wizard of Oz* cyclone. Sophie's idea of having fun is shaking her blue-and-white pom-poms at one of the boys' rugby matches with the rest of the self-styled cheerleading squad. They call themselves the All Saints 'cos our school is *Saint* John's College. Sad.

They shouldn't even be on the train — none of them actually live on the DART line — but they get their parents to drop them at Dun Laoghaire station so they can check out the Blackrock College and Saint Michael's boys on their way to school. Sad cubed.

As they pass, Seth starts singing the Oompa-

Loompa song from *Willy Wonka & the Chocolate Factory* and Annabelle scowls at him. "You're such a sketchpad, Seth Stone. Go hide behind your emo curtains." And with a flick of her hair, she continues down the carriage, coming to a stop in front of the new boy.

She smiles broadly and he looks up, stares at her for a second, then, taking off his oversize DJ headphones, asks in a deliciously smooth Northern Irish accent, "Can I help you?"

"I'm Annabelle," she simpers. "And this is Sophie. Like, welcome to our school." Then she giggles.

He looks around. "I think you'll find it's a train."

"Ha! Nice one." Seth gives a loud laugh.

The boy looks down the carriage and catches Seth's eye but doesn't say anything.

Annabelle carries on, unperturbed. "Like, what year are you in?" she asks him, batting her eyelashes.

"Second," he says, obviously deciding the quickest way to get rid of her is to answer the question.

Sophie gasps. "That's our year. What class?"

"Mr. Olen's."

Annabelle squeals. "That's, like, our class. Two O. *O* for Mr. Olen. You can, like, totally sit with us. You must be, like, so nervous, it being your first day and all."

He doesn't look too impressed. "Thanks, but I'm not in Junior Infants—I can take care of myself. Excuse me, I see some people I know. See you around." He walks down the aisle, leaving Annabelle and Sophie staring after him openmouthed, and swings himself into the seat beside Seth.

I get an instant waft of shower-fresh skin and practically melt. He's even more delicious up close and personal. Mills can't take her eyes off his bee-stung lips.

"'Pologies, folks," he says, looking a bit embarrassed. "I'm on the run from scary-biscuit D4s. Mind if I kick back with you guys?"

Before we have a chance to say anything, Annabelle and Sophie clip-clop past us, back to their D4 pack. They scowl at me and Mills and tinkle their fingers at the new boy as if nothing has happened.

"Bye," Annabelle twitters at him. "Like, see you in class."

"Yeah, see ya," he says gruffly, then pulls his lips into what looks more like a grimace than a smile.

Virtually swooning, Annabelle runs the rest of the way down the carriage, Sophie at her heels, jumps back into her seat, and starts fanning her face with her hand and whispering to the other D4s.

The boy shakes his head and sighs. "I was kind of hoping Saint John's would be D4-free."

"No way, 'cos we've, like, totally infiltrated the whole country," I say in my best D4 voice, then stop and grin. "Worse luck. I'm Amy, by the way. And that's Seth."

Seth says, "Hiya," and smiles at him.

The boy looks at Mills expectantly, who just gazes back dreamily, until I elbow her in the side. "Oh, sorry. I'm Mills."

"Hi, Mills." As he nods, his dark shaggy fringe falls across his forehead and I can see why Mills is so besotted. "I'm Bailey Otis."

"Hi, Bailey Otis," she says, her voice all breathy. "What a beautiful name. Just beautiful."

"I overheard you saying you're in Two O. We are too," I go on quickly, before Mills has a chance to say anything else. "Except Seth. He's in Two B—"

I'm interrupted by Nina Pickering—another D4—shouting from the far end of the carriage. "What's your name, new guy?" she hollers. "Annabelle fancies you."

At that, Annabelle shrieks and hits Nina on the arm. "No, I don't! Pay no attention to Nina. She's, like, totally mentally deficient. Failed all her summer exams."

"I did not!" Nina protests.

Annabelle sniffs. "Nina, an *A* in sex ed doesn't count."

"You just said he was cute," Nina protests, pursing her lips, "and that he obviously fancies you."

Annabelle's cheeks flame, and Bailey looks mortified.

"Sorry, but I'm off girls for Lent," he says. "And Barbie look-alikes aren't my bag. I like my girls *au naturel.*"

The D4s all gasp and swivel their eyes from Bailey to Annabelle, like they're watching Wimbledon and Bailey has just lobbed a tricky ball at her.

"Oops, didn't mean to say that out loud," Bailey murmurs, too low for Annabelle to hear.

Annabelle sniffs. "Barbie look-alike? How dare you? My looks are, like, totally natural." She strokes her blond curls, which are so bleached you can almost smell the ammonia whenever she tosses her head. "Well, mostly . . . And you'd be lucky. I don't do sulky music-head emos, however cute they might be." She narrows her eyes. "And you'd better, like, keep out of my way, new boy, if you know what's good for you."

The D4 eyes swivel back to Bailey.

"Happy to oblige," he says.

Annabelle gasps then gives him an evil glare, while the other D4s drop their heads into a gossip huddle and hiss, "Like, OMG, OMG, did you hear what he just said?" at each other. "So totally out of line."

After holding her death stare for a few more seconds, Annabelle lowers her head and joins them. They're like a pack of hyenas tearing strips off a carcass, their tongues going lash, lash, lash — and this time Bailey is their prey. Now and then, one of them sticks her head up out of the huddle, looks at him, and bobs back down again.

Bailey is looking pretty gloomy. "I should learn to keep my mouth shut. I've already made an enemy and we're not even in school yet."

"Look, most of the D4s are as thick as bricks," Seth says. "Just keep away from Annabelle and you'll be grand. She's a wagon of the highest order and doesn't like being made to look bad in front of her cronies. Give her a wide birth and you'll survive. Hey, you're welcome to hang with us at break and lunch. We don't go anywhere near D4ville."

Bailey smiles. "Cool, thanks. I was hoping to avoid any drama until at least my second day."

Mills giggles. "You're so funny, Bailey."

"Have you just moved down?" I ask him quickly,

trying to deflect his attention from Mills's besotted gaze.

Bailey looks confused.

"From the North?" I add.

He says nothing for a second, then, "I moved to Bray a while back. From Rathgar. Haven't lived in the North for years."

"What school were you in before?"

"Lakelands in Bray."

I sit up. "Really? I've heard it's really posh and that all the sixth-years drive around in their own BMWs. Is it true? Is that why you left? Was it too posh? Or were you expelled or something?"

Mills's eyes widen and I can tell she's dying to hear the answer.

"Amy, stop with the questions," Seth says with a laugh. (I have to admit Bailey is starting to look a little uncomfortable.) "I know you want to be a journalist and everything," he continues, "but do you have to interrogate *everyone*?"

"A journalist?" Bailey asks with interest. "Really?" I can't help noticing how relieved he looks at the shift in conversation.

I shrug. "Maybe. Or a psychologist. I haven't decided yet."

"I'd lie on your couch any day." Seth gives me a cheeky wink.

"With all your psychoses, I'm not sure you could afford to pay me for all the time you'd chew up," I say, thumping his arm playfully.

"*Touché*, Amy." Bailey grins, a smile so sunny, so involving, it almost sends Mills sliding off her seat. It even gives me goose bumps, and I have Seth, who's no slacker when it comes to magic smiles.

"What were you listening to?" I ask, nodding at Bailey's headphones and hoping he'll smile again.

Bingo! Once more his smile sweeps over us like the warm yellow beam from a lighthouse. "You into music?" he says. "Cool . . ."

Maybe this term's not going to be so boring after all.

"Stop talking!" Mr. Olen bangs a pot of blue poster paint on his desk. He's been in a bad mood all lesson — guess we're not the only ones suffering from back-to-school blues. "I said *ciúnas*! I have a message from Miss Lupin. Could all the students going on the Paris trip please meet during lunch break in the sports hall. That's in two minutes, people. Finish clearing up. And, Seth, what are those?" He points at Seth's pen-and-ink drawings.

"Skulls, sir."

"I asked you to design costumes for *Romeo and Juliet*, not *The Pirates of Penzance*."

"Play's about love and death, sir. It's bloody too — all those fights."

I look across at Seth's sheet, and sure enough, the top of his intertwined skulls is heart shaped.

"I'm going to screen print this design onto Juliet's dress," he adds. "In bloodred."

"Right." Mr. Olen doesn't sound convinced, but before he can say anything else, the bell rings and we all jump to our feet. "Quietly, please, class!" he shouts.

We ignore him and run toward the exit, jostling in the narrow doorway to get out first, our feet thundering on the thin wooden floor.

"Sneak down to the shop with me?" Seth says when we finally escape. "I'm starving."

"You have to meet Loopy, remember? About the Paris trip."

"Not going."

"What?"

"You heard me. I'm giving the trip a miss. So there's not much point going to the meeting, is there?"

I stop dead and stare at him, but he keeps walking.

"Seth! It's *Paris!*"

He swings around. "It's no big deal, Amy."

"Excuse me for being confused, because up until a few days ago you couldn't wait to get there. In fact, I had to ask you to stop banging on about the Louvre and the Pompidou Centre 'cos it was starting to bug me. I'm not thrilled about you going away without me, but I'd started to get used to the idea. What's going on, Seth? You've been in a really funny mood recently."

"Nothing. I just don't fancy it; that's all."

"Seth." I grab his face and make him look at me. His eyes are dark and his gaze shifts away.

"Talk to me," I say. "There's something you're not telling me."

He swats my hand away. "'S nothing. Just leave it, OK?"

I think for a second. It must be something pretty serious to get him into this kind of state. The last time he went all moody and quiet was when he was worrying about his mum. She had breast cancer recently, and I know the whole experience really shook him. "Is it Polly? Is she sick again? Is there anything I can do to help?"

Seth's eyes narrow. "You think life's so easy, don't you? Something happens and then you jump in and solve the problem. Well, my life's not that simple, Amy. There are some things that can't be fixed. Now, just leave me alone." He starts to walk down the drive, toward the school gate.

"Seth! Come back!" I shout after him. He ignores me. I stand and watch his back as he clears the gates, turns sharp left, and disappears out of sight.

"Seth!" I cry, but it's too late — he's gone.

♥ Chapter 5

"I finally got an e-mail from Ed last night," Mills says on the DART on Wednesday morning. We're both still puffing and panting in our seats from running for the train — Mills hates being late for school. "He cyber-dumped me."

Even though I've been expecting it, I still feel terrible for her. "Ah, Mills. What did he say?"

"That long-distance relationships don't work. He's met someone else: Kelly-Marie. She's in his class."

"I'm so sorry. I know you really liked him." I twist in my seat and give her a bear hug.

"Get a room, lezzers," someone shouts from the other end of the carriage. I swing around. It's Sophie

Piggott, of course. She's flanked by a bunch of giggling D4s who are egging her on. I poke my tongue out at her. Stupid cow.

When I turn back to Mills, she's staring down at her scuffed ballet pumps. I can tell she's trying to hold it together. Then tears start rolling down her cheeks.

"Sorry," she murmurs, brushing them away. "I feel stupid for being so upset. I should have seen it coming. Did it hurt when you broke up with Seth in the summer?"

"Big time," I tell her, thinking back to July when Seth was in Italy with his mum and met this girl called Jin. I'd gotten a bit shirty about how much time he was spending with Jin, and to cut a long story short, we broke up. At the time I was distraught. Luckily, I came to my senses and we managed to work it out in the end.

"I couldn't sleep," I continue. "I kept going over and over it in my head. I'd wake up in the night thinking about it and feel sick to my stomach." Then I realize what I've just said. Not very encouraging, Amy. "But it gets easier," I add.

"You and Seth are different," Mills says. "You're made for each other. Ed was nice and everything, but Seth's really special."

Now it's my turn to gulp back tears. "I know,"

I manage. "But I'm really worried about him. He's gone incommunicado."

Mills's eyes widen. "I thought you said he was sick yesterday."

I shake my head. "We had a fight on Monday. I just didn't want to talk about it." I tell her what happened after art, about how Seth stormed off when I asked him about Polly.

"Do you think she's sick again?"

Mills and I are the only two people in the whole school who know about Polly. Seth wasn't all that pleased that I'd told Mills, but I needed someone to confide in, and after a while (and a few grumpster days), he understood. He's very private that way and doesn't like people knowing his business. He and his mum are pretty tight—there's just the two of them—and I think Polly's cancer made them even closer.

I look at Mills and nod. "I saw her last week and she's gotten really pale again and dead skinny." I realize what I've just said—*dead*—and it sends a shiver up my spine. I bite my lip. "And now Seth's shutting me out. I just want to help, Mills, but he won't even talk to me."

"Oh, Ames, I'm so sorry." Mills wiggles closer to

me and puts her arm around my shoulder. "Here's me banging on about a silly holiday romance when you have far more serious stuff to deal with."

There are laughs and catcalls from the D4s again, but we just ignore them. Their idea of "friendship" is so tainted and warped, it doesn't bear thinking about.

"Maybe Seth just needs some time to come to terms with what's going on," Mills continues. "Is his mum going to have another operation?"

Polly had one of her breasts removed in the spring—just before Seth and I got together. She had to have chemotherapy and radiation treatment to make sure no cancer cells lingered in her body.

I shrug. "I have no idea. He won't talk to me, remember?"

"It's gotta be tough. I guess you just have to give him some space and hope he snaps out of it."

I nod. "Sorry to hit you with all this, Mills."

She bumps her shoulder against mine. "Hey, that's what friends are for."

We sit in silence then, watching the train stations whiz by—Salthill, Seapoint, Blackrock—until we get to Booterstown, our stop.

"It'll all work out," Mills says as we stand up to

get off. "He'll come around and Polly will be just fine. You'll see."

Sometimes I wish I had Mills's dogged optimism.

By lunchtime, I still haven't talked to Seth. At least he's in today — I spotted him going into French class earlier — but he's obviously avoiding me. I'm sitting at the bottom of the steps in the science block, poking glumly at my cheese sandwich. I know I should eat, but I have a lump in my throat the size of an orange and it's making swallowing almost impossible. Mills is outside with Bailey, but I'm not in the mood for being sociable.

I decide I'd better eat something and am about to peel back the skin of my banana when I sense someone is looking at me. I raise my head. Seth is standing at the top of the steps and our gazes lock. His eyes are vacant and he doesn't wave or even smile — it's as if I'm someone he used to know, not his girlfriend.

I can't bear Seth treating me like a stranger. My eyes sting, then fill with tears. Mortified that someone — one of the D4s, knowing my luck — will see me in bits like this, I wipe them away quickly with the bottom of my shirt and stand up, eager to hide my sobbing in the loo.

Unfortunately, to get there I have to pass Seth, who's still standing at the top of the stairs, not saying a word. I hang my head and start climbing the steps, tears dripping from my eyes and splashing onto the gray lino. Part of me wants him to see how upset I am — what he's done to me — and another part of me is ashamed of crying in school. How pathetic is that? So by the time I reach the top step, I'm almost holding my breath. *Nearly there,* I tell myself. Just a few more yards. Then I feel Seth's hand on my arm and, lifting my head, I look at him through bleary eyes.

His are dark, almost petrol blue, like a storm at sea, and he looks a mess. His shirt is hanging out and it's so creased it looks like he's slept in it, and there's a large inkblot on the knee of his trousers.

For a few seconds, we just stand there, staring at each other. Tears are still flooding down my cheeks, but I don't bother to brush them away now. Suddenly I don't care who else sees me — I want him to realize how much he's hurt me.

He reaches out and brushes my cheeks with his fingers. "I'm sorry. I never meant to upset you, Amy. Things have been a bit difficult over the last few weeks."

"What's happening, Seth? Why won't you talk to me?"

"I can't. It's too much. . . . I don't even want to think about it."

"Seth, please don't shut me out. I just want to help."

He gives a bitter laugh. "That's just it — don't you understand? You can't *help*, no one can *help*. And it's not fair. She's never done anything wrong. Why does this keep happening to her? I don't understand." Then he crumples against me, almost knocking me over, and clings to me like a life raft in a storm.

"It'll be OK, Seth," I say softly, holding him tight. "It'll be OK."

"Stop it, Amy," he snaps. "Don't you see? It won't be OK. Not this time."

"What are you talking about?"

He shakes his head. I make him sit down beside me on the top step.

"It's me, Seth," I whisper. "Just me and you. I know I can't fix everything, believe me. But you can't deal with everything on your own either. I'm your girlfriend, but I'm also your friend and I care about you. Can't you see that? And I'm not apologizing for wanting to help — that's just who I am. So we can sit here in silence if you like, or you can tell me what's going on. Either way, I'm here for you. Understand?"

"I'm sorry, Amy. I'm so, so sorry." He gulps and I

can tell he's trying not to cry. It alarms me a little; it's one thing for me to be caught crying in the corridor, but if the Crombies see Seth breaking down, they'll never let him forget it. (Crombies are the male equivalent of the D4s and equally as nasty.) Then I chastise myself for caring what the Crombies or the D4s think. They're raptors, the lot of them.

We sit for what seems like an age, but is probably only a few minutes, in complete silence, our heads bowed. Finally, Seth starts to talk. "One of Polly's routine blood tests came back abnormal. The doctor brought her into the hospital yesterday for more tests. Bone scan, CT of her head and body, two different biopsies. Polly said she'd be fine on her own, but I refused to go to school, so she let me go with her in the end." He pauses and sighs.

I take a deep breath. No wonder Seth's been on edge — this sounds serious. But I have to give him hope. I think for a second — what would Mills say? She's always so positive and upbeat about everything. "There's a good chance they won't find anything, Seth. They're probably just being cautious."

He snorts. "Amy, they don't do those tests for a laugh. They're seeing if the cancer's spread. They're looking for bone cancer and lung cancer and liver cancer and brain cancer." He says it in such a rush he has to stop to catch his breath. "I looked it up on the Internet. That's what all those tests are for."

"I thought Polly was on some sort of special drug to stop it coming back."

"She was. Tamox-something-or-other. But, according to the blood test, it doesn't seem to be working."

Now I really don't know what to say.

"And guess when the test results are due back," he says, his face twisting into a wry grin. "The week after next. Slap bang in the middle of the Paris trip. I have to get the results with her, Amy. She doesn't have anyone else. If it's bad news, she'll need me."

"She must have friends, Seth. Or a sister or something?"

"Polly's an only child and we were in London for years. She didn't keep up with many of her mates back in Dublin. I think she and Dad were pretty self-sufficient, did everything together."

"I know you said she's not in touch with him, but things are a bit different now and I'm sure he'd —"

Seth's back stiffens. "Don't even think about it. My dad's out of the picture, full stop."

I feel so sad for him. My own family is more the Simpsons than the Waltons, but at least there are people I can rely on if something happens, even if they do drive me bonkers most of the time.

"I could go with her," I suggest.

"Thanks, Amy. But it needs to be me."

Maybe Seth's right: if it were Clover or my mum, I'd feel exactly the same way. Seth's loyal, and that's why I love him. Paris may have to wait. It just seems so unfair; Polly saved up all summer to pay for the trip, and I know she really, really wants him to see Paris. It's one of her favorite cities — she showed us all these amazing photos she took on a fashion shoot there a few years ago and made Seth promise to visit some of the cool places she'd snapped.

"What if Polly got the results before you went," I ask, thinking out loud, "and they showed that everything was fine? Would you go then?"

He shrugs. "I guess — but it's not likely to happen. Hospitals move pretty slowly."

I squeeze his hand. "Don't rule it out yet, just in case. Look, I know you're scared, I would be too, but I have a good feeling about all of this. Honestly. I'm not just saying it to make you feel better. Your mum's really tough; you know that. There's no way she's going anywhere without a fight."

"That's just it — I don't want her to have to fight; I want her to be well again. She only told me about the blood test on Sunday night. I've known something was up for a while now, but I still had to practically drag it out of her. She said she hadn't wanted to bother me with it."

I smile to myself. So that's where he gets it from.

"She doesn't deserve all this," he continues. "She's never smoked; she walks Billy for miles every day; she eats all the right things. It's not fair." He puts his arms up in the air in exasperation.

He's right. It's not fair. Polly's a really nice woman. I look away before Seth spots the tears pricking my eyes again. I blink them back. No wonder his moods have been up and down like a playground swing. I feel as frustrated as he does: he can't fix Polly, and in this case, I can't help him. Poor Seth.

But there must be something I can do. . . .

♥ Chapter 6

"Hey, Bean Machine!"

Seth and I are walking down to the station after school when Clover pulls up beside us in her Mini Cooper. The top's down and her long white-blond hair is ruffling in the wind. "I'm off to your place to talk weddings with Sylvie. Have new clippings to show her." She pats a bulging folder on the passenger seat. "Hop in if you want a lift," she adds, moving it to the backseat. "Seth too."

We climb in and she pulls out from the curb and zips down the road. At first, Seth looks rather alarmed and keeps glancing at the speedometer. But after a few minutes, he relaxes. Clover may drive fast, but she's pretty nifty behind the wheel.

"How's Saint John's these days?" she asks us. "Monty still modeling?" (Mr. Montgomery is our George Clooney look-alike head. And, no, she's not joking about the modeling.)

"Yep," Seth says. "Still setting pensioners' hearts racing in knitting-pattern books and shopping brochures. I spotted him in the Littlewoods catalog over the summer wearing a pair of Hawaiian shorts. I hacked into the school website and posted the pic on the extracurricular page. It was up there for weeks before Peacock noticed and took it down." He grins. (He's been in much better form this afternoon, which is a relief. I know he's super worried about Polly, but he seems to have found a way of keeping it in the background.)

Clover wrinkles her nose. "Is Mrs. Peacock still the school secretary? She must be at least sixty."

Seth gives a laugh. "Yep. But the old bag sure knows her way around a computer."

As we approach Glenageary, Clover asks, "Where can I drop you, Seth?"

"He's coming back for dinner," I say quickly. "Only I haven't told Mum yet, so don't go mentioning anything until I've asked her."

"I won't say a word," Clover promises.

It turns out Polly has completely lost her appetite,

so Seth's been living on beans on toast all week. His eyes lit up when I asked if he wanted to come to our place for dinner, and I was delighted when he accepted the invite. It made me feel useful; even if all I can do is fill his rumbling stomach, it's something. Seth really likes his food, and come to think of it, he has been looking a bit skinny-jeans recently.

Mum's clearly been waiting for me to get home, because as soon as we reach the front door, she swings it open. And before I've even opened my mouth, Clover says, "Oi, Sylvie, Amy's brought her boyf back for grub. Coolio with you?"

"Clover!" I glare at her, but Mum just smiles at Seth warmly.

"Seth is always welcome." And she kisses him on the cheek. Gross! Poor guy.

Seth looks a bit embarrassed but doesn't move away.

"Come on in, all of you," Mum trills, leading us into the kitchen. "Food's nearly ready and you'll be glad to hear there'll be no food fights this evening — I fed the babies early. Evie's already in bed and Alex is playing trains in the living room — for a change." She laughs at her own joke.

I look at her suspiciously; something has her in a good mood.

It turns out I'm right, because as soon as we're all sitting down at the kitchen table Mum says, "Got a new job today. I start in a few weeks. Ta-da!" She waves her hands in the air like a conductor. She's obviously been dying to deliver her news. "I'm ghostwriting a book for a big star. It's all a bit of a secret at the moment, so until the contracts have been signed, I'll be dealing with their agent. I don't even know who the mystery celeb is. It was Monique who got me the job." (Monique is Mum's best friend.) "She got talking to their agent in the RTÉ canteen. It's very hush-hush." Mum's cheeks are pink with the excitement of it all.

"That's great, Mum," I say. "But what's ghost-writing?"

"I write a book and someone else's name goes on the cover, usually someone famous. Madonna, Jordan — they all have ghostwriters." Mum's eyes go a little starry. "Maybe I'll get to meet Madonna. Wouldn't that be amazing?"

"Last time I checked, Madonna wasn't working for RTÉ, Sylvie," Clover says dryly. "It's more likely to be some sort of Irish actress or model."

Mum's face falls a little, so I ask, "What kind of book? A novel?"

"I think so," she says. "The details still have to be ironed out, but that's not important right now. What is important is that we'll finally have some money to pay for Clover's elaborate wedding plans, and Dave will finally be able to drop the overtime and spend some quality time at home. Where he belongs," she adds firmly. (Dave's at work *again*.)

Clover throws me a look and I shrug. I know what she's thinking: Mum has seven unpublished manuscripts sitting in dusty, elastic-banded clumps under her bed. One of them was there so long the edges of the pages grew disgusting furry gray-green mold, and Mum had to throw it out. She has a copy saved on her computer, though, "in case the publishing world ever comes to its senses," she told us.

"That's great, Mum," I say again. Luckily, she doesn't seem to have noticed the exchange of glances. She's too busy singing "Money, Money, Money" to herself while slopping a huge square of lasagna onto Seth's plate with a spatula.

After dinner, Seth and I clear the table. I think he's glad it's over. Clover spent the whole time interrogating him about up-and-coming bands, comics, Xbox games, school, Polly, even me — you name it, she asked it.

"Did you have to do that?" I hiss at her while Seth's loading the dishwasher.

"What?" she asks innocently.

"I'm surprised you didn't just plonk a lamp on the table and shine it in his eyes."

She smiles. "Sorry, it's the journalist in me — I'm doing a piece on boys and their weird little thoughts for the *Goss* next month. Seth didn't mind."

"Yes, he did. He was just too polite to say anything." I turn to Mum. "Can we go upstairs now? Clover has buckets of wedding stuff to bore you with."

"Not more, Clover," Mum moans. "I'm beginning to wish I'd never agreed to get married in the first place. I wanted something simple, but it's all becoming such a palaver."

"You'll change your mind when you see what I've found for the wedding favors," Clover tells her.

"What are wedding favors?" Mum asks.

Clover groans. "Sylvie! Get with the program. . . ."

I leave them to it.

Once in my room, Seth says, "That was nice grub, Amy. Your mum's all right. And Clover's a good laugh."

"You didn't mind her quizzing you?" I say, sitting down on my bed.

"Nah. 'S been pretty quiet at home the last few days. Polly's been sleeping a lot and I was starting to forget what my own voice sounded like."

"Was Polly OK about you coming over this evening?" I ask gently.

"Sure. Said she's glad I'm getting fed properly."

From the way he's intently studying my Andy Warhol print and avoiding eye contact, I know there's something else on his mind. I wait for a second, hoping this time he'll open up.

Eventually he does. "Sorry, I'm such a downer at the moment. If you decide it's not worth the hassle and you want out—"

"Seth! I know things are tough for you, with Polly and everything, but you're not a downer. I love being with you — even when you're not on top of the world, you still make me happy."

Still staring at the print, he runs his finger over the bottom of the frame. It comes away dusty and he wipes it on his jeans. "If you like having me around so much, why are you trying to bundle me off to Paris?"

"I want you to go to Paris 'cos I know how much you'll love it and how much you've always wanted to go, not 'cos I'm trying to get rid of you. You've had a pretty tough time of it recently and you deserve to have fun. Mills's going and you know you'll enjoy it once you're there. Does Polly know you're having second thoughts?"

"Yeah, and she's not exactly thrilled," he admits. "Like you, she really wants me to go. But Polly's not the only reason I want to stay put. Do I have to spell it out? I don't have much in my life right now, and I know it's only a week, but if I go away and something happens . . . to us . . . while I'm gone . . . I mean, look what happened when I was in Rome. . . ." He tails off and blows out his breath. "Look, I don't know if I'd cope if it all went wrong. . . . It's safer if I stay here."

I'm genuinely shocked. "Where you can keep an eye on me?" I demand. "Is that what you're saying? You have a pretty low opinion of me if you think I'll be chasing someone else the minute your back's turned."

"That's not what I meant!"

"Really? 'Cos that's what it sounded like." (But maybe that's my guilty conscience talking. When Seth was in Rome, I met a gorgeous gardener in West Cork named Kit. Nothing happened, but I've never told Seth about him: it's been my summer secret.)

"I'm sorry if it came out that way," Seth says. "It's not that, honest. It's more that I feel bad for dragging you into all this Polly stuff."

"Seth, I don't mind, honestly. I just want to —"

"Don't say it, Amy."

I strangle my "help" and instead say, "Come here, Seth."

He sits down beside me, our thighs pressing together, and I trace my fingernails up the side of his neck, lightly, gently, feeling my way along his jawbone; his skin is cool and taut. I hold his face in my hands and gaze into his eyes. Then I touch his lips gently, running my fingertip over the dark-red ridges. He nips my finger with his teeth, then hugs me close, almost knocking the breath out of me. He kisses me, gently at first, tiny butterfly caresses on my eyelids, cheeks, chin, lips. Then firmer, his lips urgent, strong.

I smile to myself. Now there are two things I can do to help him — I can feed him and I can hold him, kiss him and make him forget his troubles for a second. And knowing that makes me feel a tiny bit better.

♥ Chapter 7

Later that evening, my mobile rings.

"Amy, it's Polly — Seth's mum."

"Oh, um, hi, Polly."

Polly laughs. "Don't sound so worried, Amy. I just wanted to ring to say thanks for feeding Seth. Hope he didn't make too much of a pig of himself. And he seems in much better form this evening, much chirpier. Guess I have you to thank for that too."

My cheeks glow. Just as well we're not talking face-to-face — I hope he hasn't shared *everything* with her.

"He's such a good lad," she continues. "Takes on a lot for a fourteen-year-old. I'm always telling him not to, but he doesn't listen. He worries far too much. Did he tell you about the new batch of tests?"

"Yes. Are you OK?"

It just slips out before I can stop it. Of course she's not OK, you eejit, I tell myself. But it's too late now.

She doesn't sound bothered, though. "Yeah. But waiting for the results is a killer."

"Seth said you might get them in the middle of the Paris trip."

"Rubbish timing, isn't it? I keep telling him to go anyway, but he won't listen to me."

"Is there a chance you might get them before he goes?"

"I've nagged Dr. Shine's office half to death. You never know — maybe we'll get a break. Seth deserves it and I really, really want him to go. He's been amazing with all this —" She breaks off to cough — short, hacking coughs, like a cat with a fur ball. She sounds terrible. "Sorry about that," she says, her breath a little ragged now. "I'd better go before Seth catches me talking to you and has a hissy fit. And thanks again. He's lucky to have you, Amy. It makes things easier knowing that he has someone special looking out for him."

"He looks out for me too."

"That's good to hear." She starts coughing again. "Better run." And with that, she's gone.

* * *

After hanging up, I wander down to the kitchen to get a glass of water. Dave's leaning over the sink, scrubbing the lasagna dish. He looks over. "Hi, Amy. How goes it?"

"OK." To be honest, I'm feeling a bit down after talking to Polly. She didn't sound at all well.

"What's wrong? You look like somebody's just died."

I glare at him, spin on my heels, and walk toward the door.

He comes after me, puts a hand on my shoulder. "Whoa, there. What did I say?"

"I'm going to bed," I say, shrugging his hand away.

"Is it school?" he asks. "If someone's bullying you, I swear to God I'll go in there and knock their block off."

I laugh. I can't help it. The image of Dave marching into Saint John's to confront Annabelle or Sophie is just so funny. They'd eat him up and spit out his bones.

"It's nothing to do with school," I say. "Look, I don't have the energy to go into it."

"Is it Seth? Sylvie said he was here for dinner. Said he didn't look great. Is something up at home?"

Dear Lord, he's worse than Clover. I give in. "I think Seth's mum has cancer again. She's had to have all these tests and Seth's really worried she's going to die." There, it's out, and it's a relief to finally say it out loud.

And amazingly he doesn't tell me I'm being silly or melodramatic. He just asks, "What kind of tests?"

I tell him what Seth told me and he nods. "Sounds like they're trying to find out if the cancer's spread. But it doesn't necessarily mean it *has* spread, Amy. It might be just a precaution. They'll know more once all the results are back."

"But why does it all take so long, Dave? It's so cruel making Polly wait for two weeks for the results."

Dave clicks his tongue against his teeth. "Two weeks? Does sound like a long time, all right. You don't know who her doctor is, by any chance, do you? I could look into it, if you like, see if they can speed things up."

"Polly said something about a Dr. Shine."

Dave nods. "That would be right. She's American; head of the breast clinic. Nice woman. Polly's Polly Stone, yeah?"

"Yes."

"Let me have a word with the good doc, see what

the story is. I can't promise anything—they have a lot of patients in there—but if I explain the situation and she can do something, I'm sure she will."

Suddenly, it all feels too much and I burst into tears. "Is Polly going to die?"

Dave puts his arm around me, and I breathe in his familiar after-work bleachy smell. "Amy, she's in good hands. The best. She beat it before, right?"

Mum or Clover must have told him. I nod. I'm crying so much I'm unable to say anything.

"Then there's every chance she'll beat it again. And as I said, the tests may just be a precaution. These days there are amazing drugs out there that knock those stupid cancer cells right out of the ballpark."

"Some drugs," I say. "Polly's don't even work. Tamox . . . or something."

"Tamoxifen." He pauses. "Amy, look at me and listen carefully."

He sounds serious, so I wipe the tears from my eyes and try to concentrate. "If Dr. Shine had Polly on tamoxifen, that's good news, understand? It means her cancer cells need estrogen to grow. Do you know what estrogen is?"

I nod. "We did it in biology. It's a female hormone. Made in the ovaries."

"Good woman. It means her cancer may be easier

to treat than other cancers. If the tamoxifen isn't working, there may be other drugs that will. It's one of the reasons the hospital brought Dr. Shine in from New York—she's had a lot of success with her clinical trials for other cancer drugs. I know this is a lot for you to take in, but there's still lots they can do for Polly."

I start crying again. "Why do people get cancer in the first place? It's horrible."

"I know, Amy, believe me. Every day I have to deal with the fact that horrible things happen to decent, ordinary people. That's just life, I'm afraid. And we have to make the most of it." He breathes out slowly. "Pretty heavy stuff for a Wednesday evening. You all right?"

I shrug, feeling drained but surprisingly relieved. Dave's pretty direct, and he wouldn't tell me there was hope if there really wasn't. "Guess so."

"I'll talk to Dr. Shine tomorrow, I promise. In the meanwhile, try not to worry about it too much. There's a reasonable chance Polly will be fine—the tests may come back negative."

A *reasonable chance?* My heart sinks again. I know he's only being honest, but just this once, I wish Dave could morph into sunny-side-up Mills and tell me what I want to hear.

*   *   *

The following evening, for the first time ever, I can't wait for Dave to come home. Every time I hear a car door bang outside, I rush into the hall, hoping it's him. At ten past nine, he finally walks in the door. (I can see why Mum gets so fed up with him. He was supposed to be home before eight.)

"Did you talk to Dr. Shine?" I blurt out. "Is there any news?"

"Whoa, Amy! Let me get my jacket off before you bombard me with questions. Let's take this into the kitchen, or we'll wake the babies."

"Well?" I ask impatiently as soon as he's closed the kitchen door behind us.

"The good news is Dr. Shine is going to fast-track Polly's results — Polly should have them by the end of next week. Dr. Shine says obviously she can't discuss a patient's details, but she told me to reassure Seth that she'll do everything in her power to keep Polly alive for many years to come."

I start crying again. *Siúcra*, I'm like Niagara Falls these days.

"Thank you," is all I can manage to say, but I think Dave understands.

Now we all just have to wait.

♥ Chapter 8

"Clover! Yuck! Take your finger out of my nostril!"

"Hang in there, Amy. Nearly got it."

"Ow, Clover. Ow, ow, ow!"

"Attaboy!" Clover studies the top of her nail as if it's the most interesting thing in the world. "*Siúcra*, Beanie, I just extracted the most gigantic blackhead. A whopper. Top's almost the size of a pinhead. In fact, I don't think I've ever seen—"

I groan. "I appreciate the running commentary, but you're not making me feel any better about my spots." I pick up the compact mirror and peer at the flashing red ridge between my nose and cheek. At least the offending zit is gone—even if my skin is protesting at Clover's rather violent treatment.

Clover leans toward me. "I can see more black-heads," she says, a little too gleefully for my liking.

"Step away from the blackheads," I tell her, flicking the mirror closed and putting my hand up like a traffic warden. "Go and squeeze your own spots, you freakoid."

She smiles. "Go on, Beans. Just one more. Please?"

I shake my head. "You're one sick puppy."

"Brains lets me pop the whiteheads on his back. Now that *is* fun."

"You squeeze your boyfriend's spots?" I squeal in disgust. "Gross! TMI. Too Much Information."

When she opens her mouth to say something else, I press my hands over my ears and hum "Dancing Queen" to myself.

Clover's nothing if not persistent, and grabbing my hairbrush, she jumps on my bed and starts belting out, "Squeezing Queen, feel that zit splat the window screen."

I wrinkle my nose. "Clover, that's disgusting."

But she continues, "Squeezing Queen, wipe the gunge off with Windolene, oh, yeah."

She's about to start on a second verse when Mum walks in, her hands on her hips. "Keep the noise down, girls. Evie's asleep. What are you pair up to?"

She looks suspiciously from Clover to me and then back again.

Clover shrugs. "Nothing, sis."

Mum doesn't look convinced. I hide my throbbing face with my hand. Earlier, I asked her about squeezing my spots, and she said that unless I wanted to scar my face for life not to touch them. But the one on the side of my nose was so revolting it was practically flashing like an emergency beacon — I couldn't just leave it there! So when Clover came over to go through yet more wedding plans with Mum, I asked her for advice. At the time, I had no idea she actually gets a kick from fiddling with other people's pores; I thought she was just being helpful.

"Well?" Mum demands, determined to get a proper answer. She's very stubborn, my female parental.

"Sylvie, stop with the questions," Clover jumps in, climbing down from the bed. "It has something to do with your hen night, and that's all I can divulge at this moment in time."

"I keep telling you, Clover," Mum says. "I'm not keen on hen nights. And I refuse to go anywhere near Temple Bar or wear a tiara or have anything to do with chocolate willies. And speaking of wedding plans, I can't believe you invited Monique over behind my back."

"Someone has to make you see sense," Clover says. "Your wedding day's hurtling toward you, Sylvie, at warp speed, and you've done *nada*. If I can't get through to you, maybe Monique can."

Like I said, Monique is Mum's best friend. She's an actress — sorry, actor. (She doesn't like the term "actress," says it's sexist. You don't use a different word for a female writer or singer, she says, so why for an actor?) Monique's 50 percent French, 100 percent deranged. Clover and I call her Mad Monique. Mum and Monique have been best friends forever, although when I was little she wasn't around that much. I don't think she and Dad saw eye to eye. They certainly don't now, not after the divorce and all that business with Dad and Shelly sneaking off to get married and everything.

But Monique was amazing when Mum and Dad split up and Dad moved into an apartment in town. She came to stay with us for a while on account of Mum — who was practically turning into a zombie, wandering around the house in her dressing gown, sighing all the time, not washing or even bothering to brush her hair. She was a right mess.

Monique made dinner every night and forced Mum to eat — crêpes, roast chicken, casseroles, all with loads of garlic, of course. (Monique has a thing about garlic, says she'd be dead if it weren't for her bulb a day.) She was lovely to me too and used to read me stories at bedtime when Mum was too sad to do it. *Tracy Beaker* and anything by Roald Dahl. Her favorite was an old French book with pictures called *Madeline*. It was about a boarding school in Paris. I still remember bits of it even now: "In an old house in Paris that was covered with vines lived twelve little girls in two straight lines."

I'm not sure we would have coped without Monique.

Right on cue, there's a bang on the door, and Evie starts wailing.

Mum sighs. "That must be Monny. I'll have to settle Evie. Will you get the door, Clover?"

"Coola boola. Coming, Amy?"

I follow her down the stairs. It's definitely Monique — I can see her tall, slim profile through the glass panels at the side of the door. There aren't too many women who are over six foot. Clover pulls the door open, and sure enough, there stands Monique beaming at us. "Clover," she coos, lunging forward and planting a smacker on each cheek before turning to me. Grabbing my arms, she pulls me toward her bony chest.

I'm practically asphyxiated by her signature

perfume — it's so strong I can taste it at the back of my throat. I don't know what it's called, but it smells warm and spicy, like a Christmas candle.

"Aw, my little darlings. So delightful to see you again. And where is Sylvie?"

"Settling Evie," Clover says.

"Ah, we have things to discuss . . . and if Sylvie is busy upstairs, this may be to our advantage, no?"

"Shh," Clover whispers and pulls the two of us into the living room.

Once inside, Monique kicks off her red ankle boots and sprawls on the sofa — her cream cigarette pants and buttoned shirt stand out starkly against the navy blue of the cushions, like a star in the night sky.

Clover sits next to her and takes a folder out of her bag. "Wedding clippings," she says, slapping its cover with her palm. I hover on the arm of the sofa nearest Monique — Clover's scary when she's in full planning mode — while Monique sits up a little at the sight of the folder. "What has Sylvie sanctioned so far?" she asks.

"Very little," Clover admits. "She's agreed to a cupcake wedding cake, a pink tea-rose bouquet —"

Monique puts up her hand. "Wait, just tea roses?"

Clover nods. "She's determined to keep everything simple."

"Simple, bah!" Monique tut-tuts, then asks, "Venue?"

Clover sighs. "I've made a few suggestions, but she's refusing to commit."

"Church or registry office?"

Clover shakes her head. "No decision yet."

Monique makes a guttural noise at the back of her throat, like she's being strangled. "Has she even organized the marriage license?"

"That's Dave's department. Can you check that for me, Amy?"

"Sure," I say. "I'll ask him about it tomorrow. He's at work now."

"I bet he's got it under control," Clover continues. "Unlike Sylvie, Dave's quite excited about the whole thing. He's even booked his morning suit and arranged his best man — Dr. Dan. And he's roped in the guys from his old band as ushers."

"Cool," I say. "Dan's lovely. He'll be fab as best man."

Dan is married to Dave's sister, Prue. We spent two weeks with them over the summer in a shared holiday house in West Cork. (That's where cute Kit was the gardener.) The holiday was interesting, to say the least. Prue's very American-soccer-mum — all snow-white Keds and velvet hairbands. She feeds her mini-Prues organic porridge and homemade hummus and won't let them watch cartoons 'cos she claims they're too violent. I think she found Mum's more laid-back child-rearing style baffling. They spent most of the holiday bickering about it. By the end, they had just about buried the hatchet, but Mum still wrinkles up her face whenever Prue's name comes up.

"At least Sylvie's three bridesmaids are all set for her big day," Monique says, squeezing Clover and me on the arms. "I can't wait. Any excuse for a party. There's a bit of a man famine in the drama world, so I'm hoping Dave's musician friends will be fabulous fun." She smiles dangerously.

"But we do need dresses," I point out. "I've said it to Mum a few times, but she just changes the subject."

Monique and Clover swap a loaded look. "Now that the hour is almost upon us, I think we should let her in on the secret, Clover."

Clover nods. "Amy," she says slowly, "have you ever been to Paris?"

"You know I haven't. There's actually a school trip there next week, but it's only for the French students, and unfortunately Mum thought I'd find Spanish easier."

Monique scowls in disgust. "Reeeeeaaaaaaaaally?" she says, doing that French rolling thing with the "r" and drawing the vowels out like a snake. "French is a wonderful, vibrant, sexy language—I feel deeply betrayed. But you would still like to visit Paris, yes?"

"*Absolument.* It sounds amazing."

"Meet your fairy godmother." Smiling, Monique waves her hand in the air like a wand and says, "*Ding!* Cinderella, you will go to Paris. Two weeks from today, in fact."

I stare at her in disbelief. "What? I don't understand."

Clover smiles at me smugly. "Monique and I have been planning a bridesmaids' trip to Paris for months. And last week I finally managed to persuade Saffy to run a piece on the most romantic city in the world. She's arranged two free flights and two free hotel rooms and everything."

"And I'm covering the other two flights," Monique explains. "Dave knows about it, but Sylvie doesn't. So not a word, understand?"

I'm grinning from ear to ear and making huffy "Ha, I don't believe it" noises.

"Say something, Amy," Clover urges.

"I can't," I manage at last. "I'm in shock."

Monique looks a little concerned. "You are happy, yes?"

I beam. I'm practically dancing inside, I'm so happy. "Yes! Yes! Yes! But why didn't you tell me?"

Monique shrugs. "Clover thought you might accidentally tell Sylvie. We want it to be a complete surprise — a weekend away from the babies, with her favorite girls. And a little shopping thrown in for good measure. I have a dear friend who is a dress designer — Odette. She makes such beautiful, beautiful dresses, and she's such a darling; I want you all to meet her."

"Clover!" I glare at her. "I can't believe you didn't tell me." But I can't be angry for long; I'm too excited. "We're really going to Paris?" I ask.

Monique nods.

"You're *so* my fairy godmother, Monique."

"Paris, here we come!" Clover says. She pulls me down across Monique and onto her knees and starts to tickle me.

"Ow, get off, Clover," I squeal. "I'm not three. Stop it!"

The living-room door opens. "What's going on in here?" Mum walks in and stares at us.

"Nothing," Clover says innocently, letting me go.

I slide onto the floor beside her and rearrange my T-shirt while she opens the wedding folder. "Ready to look at fairy lights, sis? I've found hearts, stars, moons, red chilies —"

"Why would I want red-chili fairy lights at my wedding reception, Clover?" Mum asks.

"To represent your and Dave's passionate and hot *luurrve*," Clover says in a deep movie-trailer voice.

Mum sighs and shakes her head. "Plain white ones will be just fine."

The following morning, while Mum's dressing Evie upstairs, I corner Dave by the stove. (Alex is playing trains under the kitchen table. As I walk into the kitchen I can hear him whoo-whoo-ing.)

"Fancy a fried egg?" Dave says, swishing an over-easy around in at least an inch of oil.

"No, thanks. And don't set the pan alight again, or Mum won't be pleased." I pause for a moment. "Dave, can I talk to you for a sec?"

"No news on Polly yet, I'm afraid."

"It's not that . . . it's about something else."

He turns around and rests his back against the kitchen counter. "I'm listening."

"Clover was asking about your marriage license," I say. "Is it sorted?"

"All in hand."

"Cool. And Clover and Monique let me in on the Paris secret last night. Are you sure you'll be OK with the babies for the weekend?"

He grins. "So they finally got around to telling you. Isn't it a brilliant idea? Sylvie's not herself at the moment, and a weekend away with you lot might just snap her out of her bad mood—stop her going on at me. You're excited about the trip, right, Amy? First time in Paris, huh?"

I smile. "No kidding." In fact, I was up most of last night thinking about the timing. It was only after Clover and Monique had left that I'd realized the implications of being in Paris in two weeks' time.

Following a lot of cajoling from me and Polly, Seth has finally agreed to go on the school trip. Which means that for two brief days, Seth and I will be in Paris AT THE SAME TIME! What are the odds?! It's fate!

And then this insane plan started bubbling away in my head: wouldn't it be amazing if I didn't say a word to him and just jumped out somewhere romantic, like the top of the Eiffel Tower, and yelled, "Surprise!"? The more I thought about it, the more the idea took hold, until I was practically squirming with excitement and anticipation. Imagine Seth's face!

So saying I'm excited is an understatement.

"I can't wait," I add. "Monique's going to show us all her favorite Parisian haunts. Oh, and I should warn you, she has wicked plans for your musician friends at the wedding." I grin and wiggle my eyebrows.

Dave laughs. "Does she, now? She hasn't seen them yet. Hope she likes beardy men—"

Suddenly, there's an ear-piercing beeping noise. *BEEP, BEEP, BEEP, BEEP.* It's the fire alarm! Flames have started leaping from the frying pan, and a cloud of intense black smoke is filling the room.

Dave grabs the handle and whips the pan off the ring. "Open the back door, Amy," he hollers. "Quick!"

As soon as the door is open, he runs outside and douses the flames with the garden hose. I look around for Alex, to make sure he's all right, but I can't see him. I'm just getting worried when he reappears from the hallway, holding his red fire truck.

"I Fireman Sam," he shouts in his little toddler voice, running toward the back door. "I save you, Daddy."

I laugh so hard I give myself a stitch.

♥ Chapter 9

Early on Saturday afternoon, Shelly walks into my attic den in Dad's house. She's puffing and panting from climbing all the stairs, and her hands are wrapped around her massive preggers tummy. "I feel a bit funny, Amy," she says.

"Probably indigestion. You had two Big Macs for lunch and loads of chips." (Shelly is addicted to Macky D's — it's one of the few things that makes her normal.)

She thinks for a second. "You're right. I should stop worrying. That's exactly what it is. What are you watching?"

"YouTube."

Shelly peers over my shoulder. "Who on earth is that? Someone famous? Nope, don't recognize him."

I pause the film and flip my laptop closed. I hate backseat viewers, especially the Shelly variety. I've been checking out a TED lecture about symmetry by an English math guru named Marcus du Sautoy. My math teacher gave me the details — not during class, thank goodness, but afterward. (My math fixation is not something I want to publicize.)

TED is an organization dedicated to the spreading of new ideas. They have some really interesting people on their website talking about all kinds of things, from black holes and climate change to robots and even spaghetti sauce (seriously!). It beats the other lame *Jackass*-inspired falling-off-a-chair/swing/bike/skis clips you normally find on YouTube.

"There's no need to hide the screen, Amy. I'm not spying on you. I'm just —" Shelly breaks off and rubs her stomach. "This indigestion's getting really nasty. I don't really feel all that great." She clutches the edge of my desk. "Do you mind if I sit on your bed for a second? It really hurts. Maybe I should lie down."

That's all I need — Shelly-cooties all over my pillow. Then I notice her face. It's pale except for her cheeks, which are glowing like two clowns' noses, and I feel a bit sorry for her.

She sits on the side of my bed and starts to rock backward and forward. Suddenly, a dark stain appears on my blue duvet cover. It spreads rapidly outward, like an inkblot, then there's a splash on the wooden floor. Gross! What is that?

Shelly gives a scared squeak. "I'm leaking, Amy."

"Shelly! Tell me you didn't wet yourself."

"Of course not. My bladder's not *that* bad. *Eoi, moi Gawd* — maybe it's my waters."

"Nah," I say, thinking that Shelly must be what happens when D4s grow up. (Scary biscuits!) "It can't be." Then something else occurs to me. "But that pain you're having . . . maybe it's not indigestion . . . maybe you're having contractions."

Shelly gasps. "You mean the baby's coming? But it's not due yet."

I shrug. "I guess it might be coming early. Evie came early too. Mum's waters broke in Tesco. She was morto! But don't panic; it takes ages. Mum cooked dinner and hung the washing up before she went to the hospital to have Evie. Have you been to the special classes?"

"Yes, but our teacher went so fast it was hard to take it all in. Plus, Art knows everything, so I haven't bothered with any books. If I need to know something, I just ask him."

I try not to laugh. Dad's clueless about babies — always has been, according to Mum.

"I'm not due for six whole weeks," she says. "Ow, ow, ow. It really hurts." She scrunches up her face, tears squeezing out of the corners of her eyes.

Then it starts to sink in. The baby's very, very early — not just a week early like Evie. And Dad's in Wexford. And Mum's out shopping. And I'm all on my ownio. This is not good. Not good at all. A prickle of damp sweat starts to creep up my back, and my palms feel all hot and sticky.

"Don't panic. We mustn't panic," I say, talking to myself as much as to Shelly. "I'll ring Dad. And when it begins to hurt, do the special baby breathing."

Shelly looks at me blankly.

"You know," I prompt, "like they show you in the classes." I demonstrate, hamstering my cheeks and puffing. *PUFF, PUFF, PUFF.* Then I stick out my tongue and pant. *PANT, PANT, PANT.* "Like that." (Mum used to practice in the kitchen, stretching her tongue right out during the pants, like an overheated red setter. You don't forget that kind of thing.) "Actually, I'm pretty sure that's just for labor," I add. "I think you're supposed to be taking deep calming breaths now."

Shelly's face is still blank.

I start to get even more nervous. She really is clueless. I need Dad here, pronto, but I don't want to alarm Shelly — she already looks terrified enough.

So, telling her to just try breathing deeply, I pick up my mobile and go out onto the landing, pulling the door shut behind me. Then I punch Dad's number into my mobile. It goes straight to messages. "Um, Dad, I think the baby's coming," I say in a low voice, my hand cupping my mouth. "Not sure what to do here. You'd better get back to Dublin, quick. Oh, and this is Amy — in case you haven't guessed." I click off the phone.

Shelly's moaning so loudly I can hear it through the wood. "Amy, Amy, I need you!" she shrieks suddenly. "I can't do this on my own. Show me the breathing thing again — I can't remember what you said. Amy! *Aagghhh*. It's getting worse."

"I'll be right there," I shout, then try Dad once more. It goes straight to messages again. I leave another voicemail — I don't know what else to do. "Dad, Shelly needs you. Right now! I'm freaking out here! Just hurry."

Siúcra, siúcra, siúcra.

I try Mum but her mobile's off too. Then I try the home landline, but again, no answer. My hands start to shake. This is serious. Where is everyone? Why won't anyone pick up their stupid phone?

"AMY!" Shelly yells.

I run back in.

Shelly's face is chalk white, and her hair is stuck to her sweaty forehead. "Is it supposed to be this painful?" she asks in a small voice. "I feel like someone's cutting me in two. I need Art. Is he on his way?"

I figure that even though my own insides are jelly and I'm struggling to keep my hands from shaking, I'd better keep her calm. "He's driving up from Wexford right this second," I say. "He said not to worry, everything is under control."

"Can you ring him back? I need to talk to him."

Oops! "Better not," I improvise. "We don't want him crashing the car."

"Oh, OK, but it'll take him ages. What do we do now?" Her face crumples and she starts to cry.

Think, Amy; think! "We'll call an ambulance."

"No!" she wails. "No ambulance. I don't want an ambulance. I just want Art." Then she really starts to sob, big heavy sobs, and she rubs her tummy again. "*Eoi, moi Gawd!* No one told me it would hurt so much."

Is she deranged? I'm only thirteen and even I know childbirth is no joke! I need help and fast. And if she won't agree to an ambulance, there's only one more person I can call on — Clover.

I ring her mobile, my hands quivering. *Ring-ring, ring-ring.* "Answer it, Clover," I whisper. "Please answer it."

But it rings out. "Hey, Clover here. You know what to do." *Beep.*

"Clover, where are you?" I hiss. "Shelly's in labor and I don't know what to do. Ring me back urgently."

Then I ring again, and again, and again, until I lose count of how many times I've tried her. It goes to messages every time. I stare down at my phone. I'm so cross I feel like hurling it against the wall. Why is my family so useless? Why can't they answer their phones for a change? I blink back my angry tears and look over at Shelly. She's rocking backward and forward, her eyes fixed on a spot on the wall in front of her. She seems to be mumbling something under her breath. It sounds like "I'm not going to die; I'm not going to die." Oh, dear God, I really, really have to get her to the hospital. Right now.

"Shelly, that's it. I have to —"

Just then my mobile rings. Trembling with relief, I go out onto the landing to answer Clover's call.

"Hey, Beanie, what's up?" she says breezily. "I have heaps of missed calls from you."

Thank you, God. Thank you, thank you, thank you. I'm so pleased to hear her voice I burst into tears. "Finally!" I blubber. "Clover, where are you?"

"In the car park at Dublin Zoo, about to visit

the new baby elephant twins. What's going on? Everything hunky-D?"

"NOOOOO! How quickly can you be at Dad's?"

"Shelly being painful? I'd love some company if you want to join me."

"No! The baby's on the way and Shelly won't let me ring an ambulance."

"Where's Art?"

"At some big-deal golf tournament in Wexford."

"Typical. Hang in there, Bean Machine—don't panic at the disco. I'm on my way. ETA: ten minutes. Over and out."

I click the phone off and go back into my room. Shelly's stopped rocking now and is staring at me, her baby-blue eyes wide and frightened.

"Clover's on her way," I say gently. "She'll take you to the hospital, and I'm sure Dad will be here before you know it."

"Good, because I think I'm dying," she wails.

"You're not dying, Shelly. Concentrate on deep breathing."

"Oh, shut up about the breathing," she snaps. "I don't know what you're on about." She takes several short, shallow breaths, which I know won't do her any good.

I ignore her rudeness—being in all that pain

can't be easy — and, sitting down on the bed next to her, I squeeze her hand until I hear a car screech to a halt outside.

"Clover!" I cry, dashing down the stairs two at a time and yanking open the door. "Boy, am I glad you're here," I gabble. "The contractions aren't that far apart now, which means the baby's on its way. But don't tell her that, or she'll have even more of a knicker attack."

Clover smiles and ruffles my hair. "Don't worry, Beanie. We'll just drop her to the hospital and the doctors will deal with everything. She's not due for yonks — it's probably just one of those false alarms. Braxton Hicks, I think they're called."

We climb the stairs. Clover seems very calm until she spots the damp patch under Shelly, then I notice she is biting her lip as she whispers, "You didn't tell me about her waters breaking, Beanie. Better get her into the hospital ASAP."

Clover's concern makes me even more worried. Shelly does look pretty bad: her face is now gray, and she seems to be having difficulty breathing. Clover grabs my arm and takes me aside. "She looks brutal. We have to keep her calm, Beanie. Pretend everything's fine, OK? This baby's going to be very premature. It needs all the time inside it can get."

I nod. "I'll do my best."

"Attagirl," she says, and then walks toward Shelly, smiles, and gives a little bow. "Hi, Shelly. Taxi's here. Which hospital, m'lady?"

Shelly manages a smile, which is a bit of a miracle. "Parnell Street," she says.

"Excellent. It's only down the road. We'll get you there lickety-split. Can you walk?"

Shelly looks anxious. "I'm not sure I can even get up."

"We'll help you." Clover crawls onto the bed and, kneeling behind Shelly, puts her hands just above Shelly's waist. "Amy, you grab Shelly's hands and pull while I push. One, two, three, *heave*."

Once Shelly's on her feet, I put my arm around one shoulder and Clover takes the other, and we help her down the stairs, taking it snail slow.

"That's it, Shelly," Clover says kindly. "You're doing fab. One step at a time."

Finally, we reach Clover's car. "We'll lie you down in the backseat, Shelly. Getting you in will be the hard part."

Shelly clutches her stomach again and takes a few slow, deep breaths. At least she was listening to me. "Oh, Christ, it's getting even worse."

"You're doing brilliantly," I say while Clover opens

the driver's door and pulls the seat as far forward as she can.

"It's a contraction, Shelly," she explains at the same time. "Like a giant rubber band squeezing your stomach in for a few seconds. Each contraction is less than a minute. Just ride the pain, let it flow over you, and remember each one will only last a short time."

I look at Clover in admiration. How on earth does she know so much about labor?

As if reading my mind, Clover grins at me. "Had to go to some of those baba classes with Sylvie when Dave was working. You don't forget weird stuff like that."

I smile at her. "You're so right. The amount of weird stuff I've seen, I'm scarred for life."

Shelly puts her hands on the roof of the car and tries to breathe through another contraction. I run inside and grab some cushions from the sofa to make the journey more comfortable for her.

"Do you have a hospital bag packed?" Clover is asking when I get back.

Shelly shakes her head. "Am I supposed to?"

"Dad can take some things in with him," I say gently, arranging the cushions on the backseat. "Now, let's get you into the car."

Getting her in is no joke—it's like squeezing a

hippo into a dishwasher — but after a lot of squealing and grunting (and that's just me and Clover!), we manage it.

Minutes later, we're tearing down the Liffey quays, toward the city center. And it's all going swimmingly until we hear a *NEE-NAW-NEE-NAW-NEE-NAW*. I look around and spot a police car in the lane beside us, its siren blaring. The Garda at the wheel waves at Clover to pull over.

"*Siúcra*," Clover mutters. She checks in her rear-view mirror, swerves left, and pulls in.

As the guard swaggers toward us we wait in nervous silence — with the exception of Shelly, who's still breathing noisily. Clover buzzes down her window and he crouches down, resting his blue-shirted arms on the window frame.

"Are you aware that you were doing sixty-five, miss? Down a bus lane." He lifts his dark eyebrows at Clover.

"We have to get our friend to Parnell Street," Clover says. "It's an emergency — her baby's on the way and she's not doing so good."

He gives a tight-lipped smile. "That's what they all say."

"But it's true," I cry, pointing at Shelly in the back. "Look!"

He peers through the gap in between the front seats, and sure enough, Shelly's face is almost green. She's dripping with sweat and moaning loudly, her eyes squeezed shut. His jaw drops. "Right, follow me." He jumps back into his squad car and peels off again, sirens blaring.

"I've always wanted a Garda escort," Clover says, restarting the engine. "I just wish it were in different circumstances. Hang on to your hats, lads." She rams her foot down on the accelerator and we power off.

I grip the edges of my seat with both hands and pray frantically in my head. *If we get there safely and the baby's OK, I'll help with Alex and Evie all the time, God. And I won't complain about it, I promise. And I'll be nicer to Shelly, I promise. Please make the baby be OK.*

We're soon tearing up O'Connell Street, the three lanes of traffic parting in the middle to let us through. "It's like that Bible story — Moses and the Red Sea," Clover says excitedly. "And I'm Moses, cutting my way through the waves." She's such a drama queen.

"Are we . . . nearly . . . at the hospital?" Shelly asks, her voice pinched with pain.

"Two more minutes," I tell her. "Hang in there — you're doing great."

♥ Chapter 10

We made it! The guard helped us get Shelly into the lobby of the Parnell Street Maternity Hospital. She's in the examination room now, and Clover and I are sitting on red leatherette seats in the waiting area, frantic to hear what's happening. I've just tried calling Mum and Dad again, but with no joy.

Clover pats my hand. "Don't worry, Beanie. Shelly will be fine."

I bite the inside of my lip. "And the baby? I should have rung an ambulance as soon as her waters broke. What if something bad happens? It'll be all my fault."

"No ambulance could have got us here as quickly as that guard," she says. "Cute, wasn't he?"

"Clover, you have a one-track mind. And you also have Brains, remember?" Then I pause. "You two haven't had a fight, have you?"

"Nah. Chance would be a fine thing. He's always away these days — festivals, weddings, gigs. His band's really starting to take off." She stares down at her left hand and twists her silver butterfly ring around and around on her index finger. (Brains gave it to her for their three-month anniversary.) "We're practically living two separate lives. And once I go to college in October, things will get even harder."

"Ah, Clover, it'll work out. Brains is mad about you."

"It's not just Brains. . . . Maybe I should leave college for another year, just stick with writing for the mag. I don't feel ready for essays and exams and stuff."

I say nothing for a second. Clover's not afraid of anything — spiders, greasy seaweed grabbing her legs when she's swimming, D4s, driving down bus lanes — but the whole idea of college seems to terrify her.

"Everyone will be a year younger than me and I won't fit in," she continues, in a *Borrowers*–small voice. "I should have gone last year with the rest of the gang from school."

"They'll still be there."

"But they won't want to hang around with a fresher, will they? They'll have their own crews by now."

"Clover, you're always telling me to be brave — 'feel the fear and do it anyway' and all that malarkey. It's time to take your own advice. Yes, I'm sure the first day will be scary biscuits, but within a few weeks you'll be running the college newspaper. You'll see."

She still looks glum. "Wish I had your confidence, Beanie."

I nudge her with my shoulder. "I didn't lick it off the stones. Everything I know, I learned from you."

Her face breaks into a grin and she tosses her hair back. "I am rather fabulous, aren't I?" Then, back to her old self again, she whistles softly and adds, "Beanie, check out that fine *fear* in the scrubs." She points at the dark-haired doctor leaning over the admin desk. "Who needs baby elephants when the men of Ireland look like that? Check out those shoulders and those buns." She's clearly spoken too loudly, 'cos he turns and looks at us.

I dig her in the ribs. "Shush, Clover. I think he heard you."

"Yikes, better stop drooling, then," she says as he starts walking toward us.

"Oh, great," I mutter. "Now he's probably going to throw us out for inappropriate waiting-room behavior."

But instead he says, "Which one of you is Clover Wildgust?"

"All yours," Clover says. Am I imagining it, or is she batting her eyelashes? She's shameless. Now is so not the time for flirting with ancients.

But the doctor just smiles, his brown eyes going all crinkly at the corners like George Clooney's. OK, I have to admit it — Clover's right: hubba, hubba.

"I'm Mrs. Green's obstetrician, Dr. McKenna," he says.

Clover snorts. "Seriously? You're a baby doctor? You're wasted on rugrats — you're far too cute, and they can't even see properly when they're born, right?"

Now she's done it! I cringe and put my hand over my eyes, utterly mortified.

The doctor laughs nervously, and I star my fingers to spy on him. He has lovely, even, Hollywood-white teeth and looks embarrassed yet amused at the same time. He clearly doesn't know quite what to say in reply to Clover's comment, though. "Um," he stammers. "Well . . ."

"How's Shelly?" I ask quickly, taking down my hand and putting him out of his misery.

He looks relieved. "She's eight centimeters dilated, so I'm going to take her straight up to the delivery room," he says, happy to be back on familiar ground. "The baby's early, but she's in full labor, so there's no stopping it now."

"Is the baby going to be OK?" I say, tears pricking my eyes. "We came as quickly as we could. Got a Garda escort and everything."

He sits down beside me on the edge of the seat. "Please don't upset yourself. Getting her here a few minutes earlier wouldn't have made any difference. And there's nothing the paramedics could have done that you didn't." He pats my hand. "Your mum said you did a great job of keeping her calm and focused. She told me you helped her breathe through the contractions."

My mum? That's a laugh. But I don't have the energy to explain.

"Some babies have a mind of their own," he continues, "due date or not. The signs are good: strong heartbeat, no evidence of distress. We won't know the full picture till after the delivery, I'm afraid. But babies are a lot tougher than you think. They're little fighters."

I nod gratefully. And then I remember what Seth said about Polly—that he didn't want her to have to *fight*. Is Dr. McKenna saying the baby's going to struggle to survive? My mind races, thinking about Shelly; her terrified gray face floats in front of my eyes.

"Any sign of your dad yet?" he asks me. "She's asking for him."

I'm too caught up in thought to answer, so Clover says, "We'll let you know as soon as he arrives. Tell Shelly not to worry; he shouldn't be too long now."

"Good. Send him over to reception as soon as he arrives. Ask them to page me." He stands up. "I need to get back to my patients now, but try not to worry, OK?"

After he's left, Clover says, "You all right, Beanie? You've gone very quiet."

"What if the baby doesn't make it?" I say, my stomach in knots. "What if it dies?"

"You heard the doctor — the signs are all good." She pushes back a wisp of hair that has fallen over my eyes. "He said not to worry, remember?"

"But the baby hasn't even been born yet. What if it pops out and it can't breathe or something 'cos it's too little?" My eyes start to tear up, and tiny beads of cold sweat dot my palms. I rub them on my jeans as the tears start streaming down my face.

Clover takes my hand. Weaving her fingers through mine, she squeezes gently. "It'll be all right, Beanie. Trust me. I know all this waiting's hard, but you heard the doc: it won't be long now."

"Where's Dad, Clover?" I say, starting to feel a little hysterical. "It's not fair! *He* should be here, dealing with all this. I feel so helpless. We're just sitting here, doing nothing. And what about Shelly? Shouldn't someone be in there with her? She's probably scared out of her wits by this stage." I pull my hand out of hers, whip my mobile out, and, ignoring the sign saying NO MOBILES, start to press in Dad's number.

"Beanie, listen to me," Clover says gently, taking the phone out of my hand. She clicks to end the call. "He's on his way, I swear. He just can't hear his phone. Helicopters are noisy beasts."

"Helicopters?" I gape at her.

 ♥ Chapter 11

Clover's right. Half an hour later, Dad runs into the hospital in his golfing gear — pink polo shirt and cream slacks — his temples dotted with sweat. Clover put in some calls on her way from the zoo. She managed to track Dad down through Felix, one of the guys in Brains's band. Felix's brother works in the sports department at RTÉ, and he just happened to be covering the biggest golf tournament of the season at, you guessed it, Wexford. He found Dad a helicopter and everything. It belongs to one of the satellite telly companies. Yeah, Clover!

The second Dad spots us, he asks, "Where's Shelly? Have I missed it? Is the baby all right?" his face ashen.

"Shelly's still in labor," Clover says. "And the doctor says everything's OK so far. But hurry. Go to the desk, explain who you are, and ask them to page Dr. McKenna."

Dad rushes up to the receptionist. She nods and puts in a call. He refuses to sit down and just paces in front of the desk until a few moments later a nurse appears through the sliding doors. "Mr. Green? This way, please. I'll bring you straight through to the delivery room."

"And the baby?" Dad asks nervously.

"Don't worry, you haven't missed the birth. But we need to hurry."

"Amy," Dad calls over his shoulder, just before he disappears though the doors, "I couldn't get through to your mum, but I managed to track down Dave. He'll be here soon."

Then he's gone.

I blow out my breath and slip down the seat. "This is all too intense. I can't bear it."

"But at least your dad's here now," Clover says. "And Dave's on his way. Good to have someone else here . . . you know . . . in case . . ." She falters.

"In case *what*?"

"In case something goes wrong. Look, it's highly unlikely, but the baby's very early and it may need special care, that's all. So Art might not be able to take you home later."

"I'm staying right here," I say firmly. "All night if that's what it takes. I can sleep in a chair. I've done it before on the ferry. I don't mind. And then I can help Shelly with the nappies and everything. You've seen how hopeless she is — she'll need me. I'll go home with them then and —"

"Amy, stop," Clover says gently, putting her hand on mine. "I know you want to be involved, but Art and Shelly may need some time alone with the baby at first, to bond as a family."

"But I'm part of their family too. Art's my dad."

"I know. But new babies have a way of taking over, and I don't want you to get upset if Art forgets you're around for a little bit once he or she has arrived. It won't last long. And you're right — down the line they'll both need your help. Anyway, for now, we need to concentrate on Shelly and the baby being OK."

"You're right — it's all this sitting around. It's doing my head in."

"I know. Let's get a Coke and something to eat. I'm sure there won't be news for ages yet."

* * *

Later, as I sit in the hospital's café, with its primrose walls and cheery servers, waiting for Clover to come back from the loo, I start to think about Seth and how he must be feeling, waiting for Polly's test results, knowing the news might be bad. Poor Seth. It must be driving him *loco*. I've only been in the hospital for a few hours and I'm already in bits.

I know the doctor said Shelly and the baby are doing fine, but I can't help feeling horribly worried. I think about ringing Seth or Mills, but I can't summon up the energy. I push away my plate of chips. It's no use: I can't even taste them, let alone swallow. I close my eyes. Dear God, I beg, please make Shelly and the baby be OK. I don't think I could cope if . . . I open my eyes. No! I can't even think it. I take out my phone and flick onto Beach Volleyball to try to take my mind off the horrible thought.

When we get back from the café, Dave is sitting in the waiting area, Evie strapped to his chest in her baby sling, Alex playing with a toy train at his feet.

Dave has a very serious look on his face. My back stiffens. Dad shouldn't have bothered calling him. The baby is going to be perfectly healthy. Why is everyone making out like something bad's going to happen?

"I came as quick as I could," he says. "Your mum's still shopping with Monique in Kildare Village, and these little monsters don't make traveling easy."

"You needn't have come at all," I snap. "Clover's here and I'm fine. And the baby's going to be fine too."

Dave looks taken aback. "I came because Art asked me to. He thought it would be a good idea in case it's a long delivery. Sometimes these things can go on for hours."

Just then a nurse walks toward us. "Dave Marcus?" She looks at Dave.

He nods.

"Can I have a word? It's about the Green baby."

"Of course. Can you keep an eye on Alex, Clover?" he says, before turning back to the nurse and explaining, "Because if it's about the baby, Amy needs to be kept up to date too. It's her brother or sister, you see."

The nurse smiles. "I understand."

"Thanks, Dave," I say, feeling a bit guilty for being spiky toward him.

We leave Clover with the babies and walk over to the edge of the waiting area. Dave squeezes my shoulder while the nurse says, "The good news is that the baby was delivered quickly and safely. Dad wants you to know it's a little girl, and Mum's doing just fine. However, there's a slight complication. Dr. McKenna and the pediatric team are with the baby now, and as soon as there's any other news, someone will come down and tell you. Dad's still in the delivery room with Mum."

"What kind of complication?" Dave asks. "Jaundice? Lungs? I'm a nurse at Vincent's. Is there more you can tell me?" Then he looks at me. "Amy, would you mind?"

It's my cue to leave. I walk slowly back toward Clover, but I can still hear them.

The nurse is saying, "She's not pinking up properly and her blood pressure's erratic."

Dave looks concerned. "Heart?"

"Dr. McKenna's ordered some tests, but yes, he thinks it's the heart."

"Is it serious?"

The nurse pauses for a second, then says, "We're not sure at this stage. But she's a strong little thing — there's every chance she'll pull through."

I gasp.

Clover looks up from playing trains with Alex on the floor. "What is it?" she asks me.

"The baby's sick," I say. "There's something wrong with her heart." My face crumples and tears start flowing down my cheeks.

Clover throws her arms around me, pulling me to her chest and stroking my hair. "Oh, Beanie, I'm so sorry."

I hear Dave's voice behind me. "You heard that, didn't you, Amy?"

I say nothing. I can't — I'm crying too much.

"Then you also heard the nurse say that the baby's strong — that she'll pull through. Unfortunately, lots of premature babies have problems. Their little organs haven't had enough time to develop. Once the test results come back, they'll be able to tell us more. Until then, we just have to sit tight and play the waiting game."

An hour later, Dave's gone home with Alex and Evie, and Clover and I are still waiting, jittery and knife-edged anxious for information. Finally Dad appears at the door.

"Dad!" I jump to my feet and hug him around the waist, starting to cry again.

"Amy, it's OK." He strokes my hair. "I'm so sorry I haven't been down sooner, but Shelly needed me."

"How's the baby?" Clover asks.

"Better. She's in the neonatal intensive care unit now, and the doctors and nurses are taking good care of her. Let's sit down."

When we're seated, Dad to my left, Clover to my right, he says, "They've run a few tests already, but it looks like she has a small hole in her heart that needs to close up. With normal full-term babies, this hole closes naturally as soon as they're born, but in the case of our little one, it hasn't happened yet."

"So what now?" Clover asks.

"They keep her in intensive care until the heart matures and closes over itself; if that doesn't happen for some reason, they give her drugs, or worst-case scenario, they operate."

"Is she tiny, Dad?" I ask.

"Yes. But she was a reasonable weight, just under five pounds, and she's a fighter. Dr. McKenna says she has every chance of living a perfectly normal life once her heart has been fixed."

Relief floods through me and I feel a little faint. "She's going to be OK?" I whisper. "She's not going to die?"

"Oh, Amy, no, no, no. Is that what you've been thinking? Come here. They're both going to be just fine." He hugs me tightly against his chest and I can feel the waffle material of his golf shirt against my cheek. It smells slightly sweaty, and piney from Dad's aftershave. After a moment, I pull away and he smiles at me. "OK, now?"

I nod. "I think so." I realize I've lost all sense of time — it's been such a heady day I don't know if I'm coming or going.

He strokes my hair. "And what do you think of the name Grace? As you know, Shelly was hankering after Wallis or Willow, but we both think Grace suits her better. Only if you approve, though."

I think for a second. "I'll have to see her first — make sure she looks like a Grace."

Dad smiles. "I'll check with the nurses, but I'm sure that would be fine. It might not be for a few hours, though. Can you wait?"

"To meet my new baby sister?" I say. "I think I can wait."

It's almost seven before I get to see her. By then Clover's gone back to our place to help Dave put Evie and Alex to bed, and Mum's sitting with me in the waiting room. She feels really bad about turning her phone off earlier. She said she'd wanted a totally child-free day. Apparently, when Dave's babysitting he's always ringing her with inane questions: "Where are my keys?" "Where are the nappies?" "Does Alex eat raisins?"—that kind of thing. But after she listened to my bombardment of panicked messages, she swore she'd never leave it off again.

"Sylvie." Dad walks into the waiting area. "Thanks for coming."

"How are you holding up, Art?" she asks.

"I'm all right now, but things were a bit shaky earlier, before we knew what was wrong," he admits. "When the poor baby's skin stayed blue . . ." He presses his hands together, puts them against his lips, and gives a deep sigh. His eyes are wet. "I was so scared, Sylvie."

Mum gives him a hug and rubs his back. They stay like that for ages, with Dad clinging onto Mum as if his life depended on it. Suddenly, I remember how it used to be, when they actually loved each other, before all the fights. For a split second I watch them hopefully — maybe they'll realize what they've lost; maybe we can all be together again — but I know it's just wishful thinking. Everything's different now, and we don't live in a fairy tale.

Dad draws away and rubs his eyes. He seems a bit embarrassed, and giving a cough, he turns toward me. "Ready to see your baby sis?" he asks.

I grin. *"Absolument!"*

We follow him down a lemon-colored corridor

that smells of bleach, up two flights of stairs, and through a pair of swing doors. He has a word with one of the nurses in the nurses' station, and she buzzes us through more doors into another bleachy-lemon corridor. Dad stops halfway along in front of a huge plate-glass window. "This is where they keep the tiny ones," he explains. "See if you can pick out your sister, Amy."

I stare through the glass at the little plastic cots inside. They remind me of the incubators we used to hatch eggs into chickens in primary school. Each plastic pod holds a baby. Some of the babies have spaghetti-thin tubes sticking out of their mouths and round white stickers attached to their chests, with wires snaking out of them. They're all wearing these teeny-tiny doll nappies, and some have white cotton beanies on their miniature heads.

I study them all carefully, and finally my eyes rest on one particular baby. She has a scrunched-up raisin of a nose, a round face with a strong chin, and a few wisps of strawberry-blond hair. There's something about the shape of her face that looks familiar.

With a start I realize she looks like me — in my baby pictures, I mean. And you know something, she's not a Wallis or a Willow or even an Amber. They all seem too flippant and Hollywood for such a serene and peaceful little tot. Grace is just perfect. Still, it's slightly too formal for such a tiny dot. It just needs one little tweak.

I point at the cot. "There. That's *Gracie*, Dad. That's my little sis."

"Gracie," Dad says, smiling. "I like that. Gracie, it is."

♥ Chapter 12

By Wednesday, things have started to calm down a bit. Baby Gracie is doing well and the doctors think she may not need surgery after all, which is a huge relief to everyone, me included.

Seth made me a baby card with "Congratulations on being a big sister (again)" written inside and a P.S.: "Hope she doesn't cry and poop as much as your other sister!" Polly's test results are due back on Friday and he's trying not to think about it too much, he says. He's putting on a brave face, but I know deep down he's worried sick.

Dad's taken some time off work to be with Gracie and Shelly—which is a first. Apparently, he took a half day when I was born (big wow!) and was back at his desk at eight o'clock the following morning. Mum has every right to feel a bit put out, but she's being very philosophical about the whole thing. "We just have to be thankful that Gracie's going to be all right," she said at breakfast this morning. "That's the main thing." But I know she's finding Dad's new-man act a bit hard to swallow.

I haven't spoken to Dad much this week, beyond a couple of quick updates on Gracie's progress. I guess that's kind of understandable, though. Shelly's still in the hospital and mobiles are banned in the intensive care unit, so finding time to ring or text me back is difficult. At least that's what I keep telling myself. To be honest, I feel a bit left out. I haven't seen Gracie at all beyond that quick glance in the intensive care unit. Dad has promised I can visit her on Saturday. Clover's going to tag along too. She's dying to see her as well. Clover's been unusually down in the dumps lately and it might cheer her up a tad. Tiny babies have a way of making you all gooey and smiley inside — or maybe that's just me.

Luckily for Seth, who is practically a basket case with nerves by Friday, Dr. Shine is as good as her word and calls Polly into the hospital on Friday afternoon. Polly refused point-blank to let Seth go with her and forced him to go to school. He's been like a cat on a hot tin roof all day, and eventually Miss Lupin let him out of French class early. (Sometimes I think the teachers know more about our family lives than they let on.)

Seth promised to contact me as soon as he knew the test results. At half five I'm sitting at my desk, pretending to do my homework but finding it utterly impossible to concentrate, when finally, *finally* my mobile rings.

It's Seth.

"Well?" I ask, my hands shaking.

"Polly has some bad cells in the same area as before, but the good news is the cancer hasn't spread to anywhere else."

I let out my breath in a whoosh. "That's fantastic, Seth!"

"I know. The doctor's talking about putting her on a new drug to block the growth of the bad cells. It's part of a clinical trial and Polly was a bit concerned it won't work, so she spoke to Dave—"

"Dave? You mean my Dave?"

"Yeah. He rang Polly last week—got her number from the hospital's files, apparently—and they've been talking pretty much every day since. Polly only told me about it today. She says he's been amazing and has really listened to her. She was able to ask him all the silly little things she didn't want to bother her doctor with."

Now I really am stumped. Why didn't he say anything to me? I'm literally speechless. Luckily, Seth isn't. In fact, he's almost gabbling. He hasn't sounded this happy for a long time. "Dave says Polly should go for it," he continues. "Dr. Shine knows what she's doing. He checked and the doctor's put Polly into the intervention group, not the control group, who just get a placebo — basically just a fake drug that does nothing. Dave says these drugs'll give her a real chance of beating this thing. So I think Polly's going to do it — which means I can go to Paris happily now and not be worrying about her the whole time!"

"Seth, that's all brilliant news." And yes, of course I start crying again. But this time they're tears of relief about Polly and joy at the Paris news.

It's been quite a week!

♥ Chapter 13

On Saturday, Dad's sitting waiting for Clover, Mum, and me in the cramped hospital hallway. He folds his paper along the creases and stands up. "Morning, girls."

"Hi, Dad." I throw my arms around him and squeeze tight.

He laughs. "Easy there, tiger." I pull away and he smiles down at me. "Ready to see Gracie?"

I nod enthusiastically. He has a word with the receptionist, who buzzes us through the hospital's electric doors, and we all troop up the stairs. (Dad hates lifts — avoids them whenever he can. He got stuck in one once in Hong Kong during a power cut, and he had to sit on the metal floor for two hours in the dark. They've given him the heebie-jeebies ever since.)

"We're like the three wise women," I say as we reach the second-floor landing, which smells of disinfectant and overripe fruit. "We come bearing gifts."

We went shopping in Blackrock on the way over, and I picked out two outfits in a baby boutique. Clover was supposed to be working on her *Goss* agony aunt pages today, but she jumped at the chance to go shopping and visit Gracie.

"Letters later, 'cos baby better," she said, laughing at her own lame rhyme. "Hey, Beanie, I'm Dr. Seuss."

Dad looks at the Bee's Knees carrier bag I'm swinging in my hand and his face drops.

"Is something wrong, Art?" Mum pants, out of breath from all the steps.

"Pauline squeezed half the baby clothes in Portugal into her luggage. And Shelly's been going crazy in Mothercare."

"Pauline?" I ask.

Dad looks confused. "Shelly's mum. I must have told you she'd arrived."

"Nope," Mum says.

"And you didn't tell *me* either," I say, a little snottily. But it's lost on him.

From the way Mum's looking at me, it's not lost on her, however. "Do try to keep in better touch, Art. We've been worried about Gracie, haven't we, Amy?"

I nod silently, not trusting myself to say anything.

"Anyway," she goes on, "if she has too many clothes already, we can always take them back and get her some toys instead."

"Toys?" Dad laughs. "The nursery already looks like a zoo, with all the stuffed animals Pauline's supplied."

"Something practical, then," Mum says tightly.

"We pretty much have everything we—"

"Art!" Mum cuts him off. "We're not the only people who will give your baby presents. Try to be a little more gracious about it the next time."

"Sorry," Dad says, but I can tell he's a bit surprised. "Didn't mean to cause offense."

Mum rolls her eyes. "You never do. Let's just give Shelly the clothes. I'm sure they'll come in useful."

We've reached the third floor now, where the rooms for private patients are (only the very best for Shelly), and we follow Dad down the corridor. A set of wooden doors, each numbered, leads off it. Now that Gracie's breathing on her own and feeding well, the nurses have allowed her out of intensive care for a visit, and when we enter room 3.8, there's Shelly sitting in a chair in a white silk dressing gown, baby Gracie cradled in her arms.

Shelly looks up and beams as we walk in behind

Dad. Wiggling out of Gracie's yellow waffle-cotton blanket is a wire, and the monitor it's attached to gives a gentle beep every few seconds. But the tube has gone from under her nose, and even in a week, she looks bigger. And her eyes are open.

"Blue eyes," I say, gazing down at her. "Like mine. Can I touch her hand?" I ask Shelly.

"Have you washed them?" a voice thunders from the back of the room.

I look up. A tall, blond woman in a tight white vest top and white jeans is staring at me. She's the split of Shelly, only older and with a deeper tan: same hair, same big piano teeth, same startled, baby-doll eyes. In fact, this woman's eyes look even wider, and her eyebrows are halfway up her forehead and peaked in the middle, like miniature alpine mountains. This has to be Pauline, Shelly's mum.

"Well?" she demands.

"Not recently," I say, my cheeks flushing. I spot a sink against the wall. "I'll do it right now."

"Mum—" Shelly begins.

"It's OK. We all will," Mum says, and she and Clover queue up behind me. "Can't be too careful."

Pauline nods. "When it comes to my precious grandchild, no, you can't."

Once we're all clean and sanitized, I'm finally

allowed to approach Gracie, and when I put my finger in her tiny palm she holds it tightly—for a tiny tot, she has quite the monkey grip.

While I'm busy with Gracie, Mum turns to Pauline. "As Art has clearly forgotten his manners, I guess I'll introduce myself. I'm Sylvie—Art's first wife."

Pauline looks her up and down, her eyes cold. "I've heard a lot about you," she says finally. "I'm Pauline Lame—Shelly's mum." She doesn't give Mum a kiss or put out her hand or anything, which is pretty impolite.

"And this is Amy," Mum says, ignoring her rudeness. "Amy and Clover were the ones who got Shelly to the hospital while Art was off playing *golf*." She puts special emphasis on the last word, just rubbing in the fact that Dad nearly missed Gracie's birth. She's always had a thing about the amount of time Dad spends on the green. "I'm sure you've heard the story by now," she adds.

"Indeed," Pauline says through tight lips. What's her problem? OK, maybe Mum's digs at Dad are a little uncalled for, but still, she's being really rude.

Mum seems at a loss as to what to say next, but thankfully Clover steps forward. "Clover Wildgust, Sylvie's sister and Gracie's aunt."

"Aunt?" Pauline looks confused.

"If Amy is Gracie's sister, and I'm Amy's aunt, then I must be Gracie's aunt too." Clover beams at Pauline, but I can tell it's one of her "don't mess with me" smiles.

Pauline sniffs. "Amy is Grace's *half*-sister — you're nothing to my Grace by blood. And I'm not sure about all this *Gracie* business, by the way. Nothing wrong with plain old Grace."

"Stop being so pedantic, Mum," Shelly says with a laugh. "And we love the name Gracie, don't we, Art?"

Dad looks up from his BlackBerry. "Sorry, missed that."

"I was just saying we love the name Gracie, don't we?" Shelly says again.

"Oh, yeah," he murmurs, lowering his head again.

"And Gracie would just adore such a cool aunt, wouldn't you, darling?" Shelly coos down at Gracie. "You'd be a lucky girlie-wirlie to have such a nice auntie-wantie."

Jeepers, I never thought I'd hear Shelly doing baby talk. Equally surprising is the fact that she's not wearing any makeup, not even lip gloss, and her hair's pulled back off her face in a simple ponytail. Having a baby has really changed her.

"Thanks, Shelly," Clover says smugly, staring pointedly at Pauline.

"Anyway, I know we can't stay long, so here are Gracie's presents," Mum says quickly to break the tension. She takes the bag off me and hands it to Pauline. "Maybe you could do the honors, Pauline?"

"The honors?" Pauline stares at Mum.

"Open them," Clover prompts. "Sylvie won't leave until you do. She has a thing about watching gifts being unwrapped. When she was a kid, she used to tear the paper off her birthday presents before the guests had even gotten in the door."

Pauline sniffs. "Is that so? I always taught my Shelly to keep her presents until after her birthday party so she could write proper thank-you cards to everyone."

"Oh, Mum, stop!" Shelly says. "I'd love to open my presents." Then she turns to me. "Would you like to hold your sister, Amy?"

I feel a rush of nerves and excitement. She's so minuscule — what if I drop her? "Can I?"

"Of course. You'll need to get in practice. I'm hoping you'll be her first babysitter."

Pauline tut-tuts. "You can't leave a teenager in charge of a newborn, Shelly. What are you thinking? And, of course, *I'll* be Grace's very first babysitter." She puffs out her chest. "I intend to stick around for quite some time. At least a month."

Dad looks up from his BlackBerry. He heard that all right! His shocked face is a picture.

"I know, Mum, but right now, Amy's going to hold Gracie," Shelly says brightly. "Now, sit down and get comfortable, Amy, and I'll pass her to you. Her head's pretty floppy, so you have to support it with your arm. Oh, and watch the heart-monitor wire."

I sit down and Shelly passes Gracie over. She's ultra light, like a doll. I support her head in the crook of my arm and gaze down. Her eyes are closed now, tiny purple veins running over the lids like road maps, and I can see her chest rising and falling under the yellow swaddling blanket. Her skin is reddish pink, and blue veins throb at her temples. She looks so wee, so vulnerable. I lower my head a little and breathe in her scent; she smells delicious, fresh cotton mixed with vanilla.

"She's beautiful," I whisper, tears springing to my eyes. "She's a little miracle, Dad."

But Dad's too busy fiddling with his BlackBerry to notice.

"That she is," Mum says, hunkering down and staring at her. She smiles at me. "And you're a natural, Amy. You've always been brilliant with babies."

"Now, let's look at these famous presents," Pauline

says loudly, making Gracie's eyelids flicker. (I think Pauline likes being the center of attention.)

"Hush, now," I say to Gracie, rocking her gently. She goes back to sleep.

"Presents!" Pauline says again, handing the bag to Shelly, who sits down on the side of the bed and begins to peel back the tissue paper carefully. She pulls out the hat and three pairs of baby tights and smiles. "Tights. How useful. And what a cute little hat." It's red with a green top, like a strawberry.

"They're from me," Clover says.

Shelly sets them down on the bed beside her and then smooths and folds the tissue paper neatly. "Thanks, Clover."

Meanwhile, Pauline has picked up a pair of the tights and is examining them, rubbing the wool between her fingers. "Can these be exchanged? I'm not sure they're soft enough, and my Grace might be allergic to wool."

"Mum!" Shelly frowns at her. "I'm sure they'll be just perfect." She opens the next parcel—pink corduroy dungarees and a striped navy-and-white sailor dress in soft cotton jersey, with matching knickers to go over Gracie's nappy.

"Do you like them?" I ask nervously.

"Love them," Shelly says. "The dungarees are so

cute. And the little sailor dress will look darling. Maybe she'll be big enough to wear it on Christmas Day."

I'm touched. That's a really nice thing to say. I know we haven't had the best of starts, but I'm beginning to warm to Shelly.

"But my Grace will be wearing the red velvet dress with the Portuguese lace collar, darling," Pauline twitters. "Don't you remember? I chose it especially."

"She can wear both," Shelly says diplomatically. "She's bound to need at least one change."

"But you'll put her in the velvet for the photographs." Pauline's not giving up without a fight.

"Mum!" Shelly says again.

Pauline sniffs. "I'm just saying . . ."

"Well, don't." Shelly opens the cards. The one from Mum and Dave has a Mothercare gift card tucked inside. She reads the messages and smiles. "Thanks, all of you. They're wonderful presents. And the gift card's really practical."

Gracie's eyes are open again and Shelly holds up the sailor dress. "Look, Gracie-gru," she says. "Isn't it cute? Art? What do you think?"

Dad is still standing by the window, staring at the screen of his BlackBerry.

"Art!" Shelly doesn't look pleased. "Put that thing down and come and look at the presents."

He raises a hand but doesn't look up. "Just a second. Something important's happening in the markets."

"More important than your own daughter?" Shelly says. "ART!"

Gracie jumps and gives a little mewing cry. This time Dad looks up. I rock her again and she stops and goes back to sleep.

"I think it's time to go," Mum whispers.

"Exit stage left," Clover adds. "Better give the baby back first, Amy."

I sigh. "Can't I keep her? She's so cute." Standing up carefully, I hand her back to Shelly. "Thanks for letting me have a cuddle. And as soon as she's home, I'll come and stay with you and help out. Give you a rest."

Pauline gives me a snooty look down her nose. "But I'll be there, Amy, so they'll hardly need your help. Besides, I'm not sure where you'll sleep, as I'm in the only spare room." Her lips curl when she says the word "help," and I feel my stomach clench in anger. What a hag! And she must know that's my room.

"That's only temporary," Clover says firmly. Pauline looks at her and they lock eyes. She's picked the wrong family to mess with.

"That sounds lovely, Amy," Shelly says, glaring at

Pauline. "And thanks so much for the presents. Don't worry, I'll be sure to write you all proper thank-you notes," she adds with a wink.

As soon as we're out of earshot and walking back down the stairs, Clover says, "That Pauline woman is as territorial as a She-Rex. Did you see the looks she was giving you, Beanie? Jealous of a teenager — what's she like?"

"Jealous of what, exactly?" I ask.

"Of all the fuss Shelly was making of you," Clover says. "And all the 'Amy's brilliant with babies' stuff. And the way you were able to soothe Gracie back to sleep. Must have put her nose out of joint. Shelly's not normally so nice to you."

"That's a bit unfair, Clover," Mum says. "Shelly has always tried to be nice to Amy."

Clover snorts. "Hello! She nicked Amy's last bedroom and painted it yellow. Made it into a nursery behind Art's back, remember? Since when are you on Little Miss Perky's side?" Clover pauses. "But I guess she was being a bit less painful than normal today."

Personally, I think Shelly was being really sweet — Dad was the useless one, but I keep my mouth shut.

"Having a baby changes you," Mum says quietly.

127 ♥

"I feel a bit sorry for Shelly. Art isn't exactly being very attentive. And imagine having a mother like that."

"No kidding," Clover says. "Did you see Pauline's pillow cheeks? Filler-rama. She's obviously been playing around with Botox too."

"How can you tell?" I ask, intrigued.

"I-spy-the-Botox-addict is Saffy's favorite game. She can't look at a celeb photo without picking over the enhanced features. If Shelly's going on thirty, Pauline must be, what, late forties, early fifties? No one has baby-smooth skin at that age. And according to Saff, Spock eyebrows are a dead giveaway. Plus, the woman has no frown lines or crow's-feet. You're years younger, Sylvie, and you have crow's-feet."

"Thanks for reminding me, Clover." Mum touches the corner of her left eye. (She's a bit sensitive about her wrinkles.)

"And did you see her rocket boobs?" Clover grins. "Can't be natural."

"Clover!" Mum says.

"What? I'm just saying."

I grin. "Thanks a lot, Clover. I won't be able to stop staring at her chest now. Checking her out for falsies."

Even Mum has to laugh.

♥ Chapter 14

Clover switches on her laptop then swivels around in her black leather chair. We're sitting in her "office," a customized shed in the back garden. Truth be told, I'm lolling on her sofa rather than sitting. Clover treated me and Mum to lunch at Eddie Rocket's in Blackrock on the way home from the hospital, and I'm still so full from my mega burger, onion rings, and curly fries I can hardly sit upright!

"So what's it to be, Beanie?" she asks, pulling some papers out of a plastic folder and flicking through them. "Boyfriend blues, embarrassing mums, or moving school?" She hands the problems over and I scan them all. One catches my attention immediately:

They've put my name first—yeah!

Dear Amy and Clover,

Please save me! My mother's a nightmare. Last night I caught her dancing in the kitchen to the Killers. She was holding her nose and twisting her body up and down like she was pole dancing . . .

"Embarrassing mums," I say firmly, looking up from the letter. "It'll be a cakewalk."

Clover grins. "No kidding, with Sylvie as your parental." She stands up. "Take the hot seat and type away."

"On my own?"

"Sure. You're ready, Beanie. And, as you say, this one will be easy peasy. I'm going to start sorting out clothes for Paris."

I bite my lip. *Paris.*

"What's wrong? Spit it out, Beanie." She knows me too well.

"What if something happens to Gracie while we're away? Something bad."

"You heard Art. She's doing really well. Nothing's going to happen."

"You don't know that for sure, and we'll be so far away. . . ."

"Look, it's all booked and we'll only be gone three days. When are you seeing Gracie again?"

I shrug. "Not sure. Dad didn't say."

"Ring him. Ask if you can visit before we leave on Friday. Tell him about the trip, but make him swear not to breathe a word to Sylvie. It's normal to worry, babes. Shows you care. But Gracie is in good hands at Parnell Street. And you can ring your dad every day to check up on her. She's only tiny; she won't even notice you're gone, honest."

I nod. I feel a bit better about it now. "Thanks, Clover."

"Anytime, Bean Machine. Now, back to Paris. How many suitcases are you bringing?"

I giggle. "Suitcases? Clover, we'll only be there for a few days."

She pretends to look shocked. "But it's Paris, Beanie: Fashion Central. We have to look our best. Now, where did I put that fake Chanel bag?" She walks off, mumbling to herself about berets and striped T-shirts.

"You're going to look like an onion seller!" I shout after her, but she's lost in a fashion haze.

I sit down in her chair, which is still warm from her bum and so feels a bit weird. It reminds me of the heated seats in Dad's Mercedes — if he turns them up too high, I always feel like I need the loo. It's a most peculiar sensation. *Dad.* His face swims in front of my eyes.

I have this other worry: maybe now that he has Gracie, he won't have time for me anymore. Maybe we'll end up drifting apart, like Sophie Piggott and her dad — she only gets to see him a few times a year since he had kids with his new wife. No wonder she's so bitter and twisted.

I tell myself I'm being silly. I saw Dad earlier and everything was perfectly normal. Yes, he was a bit preoccupied and we didn't get to talk much, but with Gracie being sick and everything, that's understandable. I need to stop being such a worry bug. Taking a deep breath, I decide to snap out of it. I have to concentrate on answering the agony aunt letter, so I knuckle down to work.

Dear Amy and Clover,

Please save me! My mother's a nightmare. Last night I caught her dancing in the kitchen to the Killers. She was holding her nose and twisting her body up and down like she was pole dancing or something. So embarrassing! (And why was she holding her nose? Supa strange!)

That's not all. I went shopping with her last week in Dundrum — nevs again. She kept dragging me into shops, holding up these really gross clothes, and saying, "This would really suit you, Romie." *As if!*

Everyone was laughing at me. And she was doing that bum-wiggling thing again in Penneys — to a Beyoncé song. Morto cubed. But at least she didn't hold her nose, I guess.

I don't mind hanging out with her some-times — she's not the worst — but I can't go to Dundrum with her again. Eva! It'll ruin my rep. How can I tell her this without being mean?

'Rents! They mean well, but they're, like, so sad.

Ta!

Romie, 14, Malahide XXX

Dear Romie,

Join the club! My mum's a bum wiggler too. And that nose-holding thing — it's a weirdo dance the olds do: imitating going underwater or some-thing. Nothing to worry about. At least she's never moonwalked across Zara. Or zombie danced to "Thriller" at your eleventh birthday party, like my female parental. Cringe-a-rama!

She probably has no idea that she was killing

your rep in Dundrum. But as she's also holding the fashion purse strings, here's what I'd suggest:

1. Go to Dundrum dead early to avoid being spotted.
2. Teach her some "normal" dance moves — if you can. Otherwise, sign her up for a dance class.
3. Suggest other things to do together — movie, pizza, a show — it might be less stressful.

And if all else fails — wear dark glasses!
Best of luck with it, Romie. We hear your pain.
Your fellow sufferers,
Amy and Clover XXX

I'm just saving the letter and wondering if Clover will notice the order of the names when she bounces in the door, like a human pogo stick. "Hey, Beanie. How did you get on?"

"OK, I think."

She sits on the side of the desk and reads the screen. "Sweet reply. Short and to the point. Attagirl.

I'll make a journo of you yet." She stops for a minute and looks at me. "You still seem a bit down in the dumps. Anything else you want to talk about, babes?"

I shake my head and focus on the bright screen of Clover's laptop. "Not at the moment."

"Coola boola. Whenever, Beanie."

I'm glad she doesn't press me.

"But remember, I'm here for you, doll face," she adds. "Underground, over ground, wombling free. Don't ever forget that."

"Wombling free?" I scrunch up my nose. "What are you on about?"

She laughs. "*The Wombles* — Sylvie's fave show for years." She reaches over and clicks into YouTube, and we watch a bunch of tubby gray bear things bumble around the screen, singing and picking up litter.

I giggle. "They're ridiculous, Clover!"

She grins. "Wait till you see *Bagpuss*. And *The Clangers*. And *Noggin the Nog*. Oh, and *Crystal Tipps and Alistair*."

I shake my head. "Weird seventies brainwashing. No wonder Mum's so strange."

♥ Chapter 15

On Sunday afternoon, I poke my head into the living room. Mum's struggling to get Alex into a long-sleeved T-shirt: as soon as she gets one arm in, he pulls it straight back out again. "Mum, I'm just popping over to Mills's to say bye. She's off to Paris in the morning. Won't be long."

I'm in the middle of closing the door behind me when Mum says, "Not so fast, Amy. Come here for a second."

"Need a hand with the toddler octopus?" I grin.

"Please. He squeezed a whole carton of apple juice over himself a few minutes ago. I told Dave not to give it to him, but oh, no, he knew better."

I hold Alex's chubby torso. As soon as Mum manages to get one arm covered, I grab his hand to stop him reefing it out again. "Busted," I tell him as he tries to shake away from my pincher grip.

Once he's dressed, Mum turns on his battery-powered Brio train and he's instantly distracted. "Shoe-shoe," he says, following it along the wooden tracks. He hasn't quite gotten the whole "ch" thing yet.

Mum flops down on the sofa. Her cheeks are flushed. Dressing Alex is a major production: Mum calls it the squiggle-and-squirm waist twist. She claims it's one of the stay-at-homers' many daily gym workouts, along with the hanging-up-the-washing arm stretch and the lifting-toys-off-the-floor leg squat.

"You saw Mills last night," she points out. "I thought you had an essay to do for tomorrow."

"It's nearly finished." I cross my fingers behind my back. (I haven't exactly started yet, but it's only three copybook pages on the Roman army. I'll fly through it, especially if I use extremely large writing.) "And I won't see her for a whole week," I moan. "Pretty please?" I kneel on the ground, press my hands together, and plead.

She laughs. "Oh, go on — if you must. You have had quite a time of it recently, what with Gracie and everything. I guess you deserve it." She stops for a second. "You haven't been given much credit for what you did for Shelly, have you? I dread to think what would have happened if you hadn't been there. I guess Art's too wrapped up in his own world to think about anything else. What's new? But you know *I'm* really proud of you, Amy, don't you?" She goes to hug me but I back away.

"I'm not four, Mum. Less with the hugs, OK?"

She looks a little upset, so I say, "Oh, go on, then. Just a swiftie."

And the next thing I know I'm squashed up against her chest. Yikes! I draw away as quickly as possible. "See you later, Mum."

"Back by six for family dinner. Understand?"

"Total comprende," I say, running out the door before she changes her mind.

As I walk toward Mills's house, I think about what Mum just said. She's right: Dad's never thanked me or Clover for getting Shelly to Parnell Street. Neither has Shelly herself, for that matter. I stop outside Mills's house, lost in thought.

Mills swings open her front door. "Hi, Ames. What are you doing standing there like a lemon? Come in."

Trying to get Shelly and Dad's ingratitude out of my head, I follow her inside and sniff. Yum! Warm, sweet . . . chocolate! "What's that smell?" I ask, hoping I already know the answer.

Mills's eyes twinkle dangerously. "Mum's choco-late brownies. Want one?"

"Is Johnny Depp a god?" I close my eyes and put my hands out in front of me like a zombie. "They're calling me. I'm coming, my choco friends. Hang in there."

Mills giggles. "If you don't open your eyes, you'll bump into something."

Sue looks over as we walk into the kitchen. "Hi, girls. Wonder what you two are after!" She gives a tin-kling laugh. She's wearing a red spotty apron, and in her oven-mitted hands, she's holding a fresh tray of brownies, their crispy tops still sizzling from the Aga. She puts the tray down on the stove and begins to cut them into wedges the size of iPods. Once she has fin-ished, she levers the slices carefully onto a plate and plonks it in the middle of the kitchen table. The aroma makes my mouth water and my taste buds tingle.

"Long time, no see, Amy," she adds with a grin. "I really don't know what the two of you find to talk about. Anyway, tuck in. You may as well while you can. All that youthful energy burns off the calories. Sadly, I'm not so lucky." She pats her curvy hips.

"I thought the brownies were for the Barnards, Mum," Mills says. (The Barnards are her host family in Paris.)

"I did two batches," Sue says. "The second lot has just gone into the oven. Come and get me when the timer pings." She bustles out of the door, still in her apron. She wears it all the time; she uses the front pocket as a handbag — it sticks out from her tummy like a joey's pouch. There are all kinds of things in there — mobile, notebook, silver pen she won in an *Irish Times* crossword competition (she's very proud of that fact), Mills's school timetable, shopping lists. When Mills and I were little, she also used to carry around a big bag of jelly snakes and dole them out when we were feeling blue. Actually, I think that was just me — the feeling-blue bit. Mills is pretty sunny most of the time, and if she ever does get down in the dumps, it rarely lasts long.

I spent a lot of time in Mills's house when Mum and Dad's marriage was going through its death throes. Even before that, I stayed over sometimes — weekends mainly, once as long as ten days — when Mum and Dad traveled without me. Dad preferred "adult" holidays for just the two of them, and Mum played along to keep him happy. (I wonder what he'll do now that Gracie is around. . . .)

As soon as Sue's out of the room, Mills rolls her eyes. "My suitcase is going to burst at the seams with presents for the Barnards. As well as the chocolate brownies, Mum wants me to bring them Jameson Irish whiskey and a *whole* Irish salmon. I drew the line at Barry's Tea. I refuse to hand Madame Barnard a box of tea bags. I hope the family is nice after all this."

"Won't the whiskey bottle smash in your luggage?" I ask.

"She's mummified it and the fish in layers and layers of bubble wrap. I know she's only trying to be nice, but I do wish she'd just give them something normal like a box of chocolates. I bet Annabelle Hamilton's mum isn't making her lug alcohol, a whole flipping fish, and homemade brownies across the Channel."

I smile. "Probably not. But your mum's brownies are pretty spectacular." My hand hovers over the plate. Then I remember something we used to do when we were kids. "Hey, Mills — one, two, three, four, I challenge you to a brownie war. On your marks, get set —"

"Wait," she cries. "That's not fair. I wasn't ready. Start again." She puts her own hand out, touching mine, and our palms jockey for space. "First to finish one," she says.

I chicken wing my arms and go "Bwock-bwock-bwock-bwock" like a giant rooster.

She eyeballs me. "Fine. First to three. But I'll

blame you if I barf on the plane. On your marks, get set, BROWNIE WAR!"

I grab a brownie and take a huge bite, my teeth sinking into the dense, silky chocolate center. I groan. "*Mamma mia*, these are good!"

Mills wipes crumbs away from her mouth. "One down, two to go." She picks up her second.

I cram the remainder of the first into my mouth and then swallow it down. (It's so delish!) Then I begin to wolf down the second. I'm just chewing the last mouthful of the third when Mills yells, "I win!"

She grins, delighted with herself, a dark-brown ring around her mouth.

I shake my head and swallow. "I must be losing my touch. Any chance of a glass of milk?" I prop my bum against the kitchen table.

As she's standing at the counter, pouring milk from the fridge into two glasses, I say, "Mills, there's something I have to tell you — something important."

She stops pouring, the carton poised in midair, and looks over. "Is it Seth?"

"No."

"Bailey? Which reminds me, I must text him to say *au revoir*."

"No!"

Mills looks puzzled. "Ed?"

"It's not about boys, OK? Jeez, Mills, talk about mono-minded. And you have to promise not to freak out."

Mills's eyes saucer. "What is it? Sounds serious."

I shake my head. "I'm not telling you until you swear you won't freak."

Mills giggles. "I won't freak, Amy. I'm the epitome of calm. Always."

I try not to laugh, and raise my eyebrows. "Really?"

"Fine," she says, a little grumpily. "I swear on Johnny Depp's life. That good enough for you?" She crosses her chest with the hand not holding the milk carton and then starts to pour again.

I smile. "*Mais oui*, my friend. Right, you're not going to believe this, but I'm Paris-a-go-go. I'm red-eyeing out on Friday morning and staying until Sunday evening."

"No!" Mills cries.

"Yep. I was going to surprise you by just turning up at your host family's house or something, but I need your help — Mills, the milk!"

She looks down. Her jeans are streaked with white and there's a puddle of milk on the tiles at her feet. "Oops," she says, putting the carton down on the counter and mopping up the mess with paper towels. When she's done, she dabs at her jeans. "Seriously?

You're coming to Paris next weekend? This isn't a joke?"

"Seriously. Me, Mum, Mad Monique, and Clover. Monique and Clover have arranged everything — flights, hotel in Montmartre, even a special bridesmaid-dress shopping trip. Isn't it fan-daby-dozey?"

Mills squeals and claps, splattering the milk everywhere again, while I grin. "I knew you'd go mental. But you can't breathe a word to Mum. We're keeping it a secret until the morning of the flight. And you can't tell Seth either."

Mills looks confused. "Your mum, I get. But why haven't you told Seth?"

"I want him to walk around the corner some-where — I haven't quite worked out where yet — and just bump into me. I can't wait to see his face. He'll be so surprised."

Mills's forehead crumples. "Shocked, more like. Are you sure it's such a good idea? Some guys aren't all that hot on surprises. And he's been through a pretty tough time recently."

"He'll love it," I say confidently. "With Polly's new treatment starting and everything, he's almost back to his old self. He'll really appreciate a good laugh." (Seth said I could tell Mills about the clinical trial, but that was it. He said he'd tell Bailey himself.)

"If you're sure. . . . You'll have to pick somewhere really romantic, like at the top of the Eiffel Tower," Mills says dreamily. Then she pauses, biting her lip. "But how will you know where he is?"

I smile. "That's where you come in, spy kid."

By seven o'clock that evening, Seth's strong arms are wrapped around me in the sitting room. He obviously had a shower just before he came over, 'cos his skin smells fresh and lemony, and the ends of his hair are still a little damp. He's holding me so tightly and has told me so many times how much he's going to miss me that I'm starting to have serious second thoughts about keeping my Paris trip a secret. Maybe Mills is right: maybe I should just tell him right now.

"I'll miss you, Amy," he says softly into my hair. "So much."

"It's only a week," I say, feeling terrible about lying to him.

He loosens his embrace, draws away a little, and strokes the side of my face with his hand, his fingers cool against my flushed cheek. "I know, but I wish you were coming too. So we could see Paris together." He blows all the air out of his mouth in a feathery sigh. "That would be incredible."

I take a deep breath. OK, I can't do this. I have

to come clean. So for the second time today I say, "There's something I have to tell you."

He gazes at me, his sky-blue eyes making me melt as usual, and then the *Star Wars* theme tune rings out. He whips out his mobile and looks at the screen. "Polly. Do you mind if I take this?"

"Of course not," I murmur.

He moves to the other side of the room and talks quietly, but I can still catch some of the conversation. "Bread, milk . . . anything else? Sure you don't want some chocolate? . . . OK, be back soon. . . . Love you too. . . ."

I smile to myself. Seth is so sweet to his mum. It doesn't sound like anything important and I'm relieved. Whenever I ask about Polly, he always says, "She's doing good," and sometimes I think his standard answer is just a defense mechanism so I won't ask any difficult questions.

"Sorry 'bout that," he says, coming over. He takes my hand and draws me in, close again. "There's something I want to tell you too." His lips curl into a tiny smile and for some reason his cheeks have gone red. "I—"

"Amy!" Mum cries, suddenly bursting in, looking flustered. "There you are. Oh, hi, Seth. Sorry to interrupt you two lovebirds, but Alex just peed all over Evie's hair and I can't find the baby shampoo. Any idea where it is?"

I'm trying not to laugh. "Did he do it on purpose?"

"I don't know," Mum snaps. "Does it matter?"

"I was only asking," I say huffily. "It's hardly my fault Alex used Evie's head as a toilet."

"Sorry, sorry. Everything's going wrong today. I'm just . . . I just can't . . ." Mum tails off and her eyes start to water. Oops, Mama Meltdown. I'd better get Seth outta here, pronto.

Luckily, Seth is on my wavelength. "I'll see myself out," he murmurs. "I'll give you a call later, Amy."

I nod, mouthing "Sorry" at him over Mum's shoulder. He just smiles at me and lifts his hand up in a "don't worry about it" kind of way.

Once he's gone, I turn back to my now-sobbing mother. "Did you check the swimming bag?"

She shakes her head, her tears splattering the carpet. "Why didn't I think of that, Amy? I bet you're right."

"I'll go and check, then you can wash Evie's hair while I deal with Alex."

"Thanks, Amy."

Just before eleven, my mobile beeps. It's a text message from Seth. We already said our final good-byes on the phone earlier. It wasn't easy keeping the secret: when he told me, yet again, how much he'd miss me, I almost blurted it out, but I stopped myself just in time. I couldn't tell him something like that on the phone, so in the end I left it.

LK OUT UR WINDOW, the message reads.

My window? What's he on about? I consider ignoring it—I'm all warm and snuggly under my duvet, rereading *Twilight* for the third time—but, hang on, what if he really is outside? I jump out of bed, run to the window, and pull back the curtains.

I rub my eyes and stare down at the road that is glowing orange in the streetlight, half expecting to see Seth waving up at me. Nothing. My eyes sweep toward the pavement. Again nothing. I'm disappointed.

I'm about to text back, asking him to explain his cryptic message, when I notice something white on the pocket of grass Mum laughingly calls "the front lawn." Leaning forward and squinting up my eyes, I can just about make out something: a white shape on the grass. It has a wobbly top and a pointed end. Hang on a minute, it looks like . . . it is—a heart! There's a big heart in the middle of the lawn.

I instantly feel a popping sensation in my tummy, like it's full of fizz bubbles from a glass of Coke, and my mouth bananas into a wide grin. Seth created a giant heart just for me. How cute can you get? I can't wait to thank him — maybe he's still down there.

I pull on my runners and creep down the stairs. The house is deathly quiet, apart from a few hicks and gulps from Evie and Alex's open door. (Evie hiccups in her sleep.)

It's breezy outside and there's a chill in the air. I wish I'd thrown a hoodie on over my pajamas. Hugging my chest, I crunch over the gravel and onto the lawn, looking around all the time — but there's no sign of Seth.

I'm standing at the edge of the heart now. What on earth is all the white stuff? It looks like bits of tissue paper crumpled up into little balls. Crouching down, I touch the heart with my fingers, just as a gust rolls some of the pieces across the grass. Hang on, I know exactly what it is. It's popcorn! And it's already starting to blow away — the right side of the heart is loose and baggy. And once the hungry morning birds gorge on it for breakfast, it'll have no chance. But maybe it's just as well: Mum and Dave would never let me hear the end of it.

I take one last look around for Seth and then, shivering, go back inside. Seth hearts me! SETH HEARTS ME! Lying in my bed, warming up under the covers, I text Seth back. I HEART U 2! AMY XXX

♥ Chapter 16

School is weird on Monday without Mills and Seth to hang out with, and by lunch break I'm starting to feel like a stray dog. From the minute I stepped onto the DART this morning, I felt lonely, a dull ache that seems to be lasting all day. It's the first time they've both been out together. Seth's often off school, but Mills is rarely sick, and even when she is, she soldiers on, battling through coughs, colds, and chest infections that most of us would use as an excuse to wallow in bed. (In primary school she won the prize for best attendance, year after year.) She hates missing classes; she thinks it'll ruin her academic career. She's aiming high — medicine — and with her tenacious work ethic, she'll get there too.

"What's wrong, Green?" says a voice. (I'm sitting on the steps outside the biology lab.)

I look up. Sophie is standing in front of me, hands on her hips. Nina and some of the other D4s are sniggering behind her. (Annabelle's in Paris, so Sophie's in her element as D4 Queen Bee for the week.)

"All your ickle weirdo friends leave you all alonio? So tragic. Why don't you join the chess nerds? You'd fit in beautifully." Sophie pushes my shoulder, hard.

"Leave me alone," I mutter, slapping her hand away.

"Ah, there you are, Amy." And Bailey comes up behind me.

"Why are you bothering with this loser?" Sophie asks him.

Ignoring her, he says to me, "Heading outside?"

I nod gratefully, and picking up my bag, I follow him past the D4s and down the corridor.

"We'll catch you later, Green," Sophie says, her voice threatening. "Oh, and does Stone know you're two-timing him? Annabelle won't be happy either. You know she has her eye on Otis."

"I'm not interested in Annabelle, or any Saint John's girl," Bailey says, walking away quickly. "And you can tell her that."

Once we're safely outside, I say, "Thanks, Bailey."

He shrugs. "'S OK. Thought we could hang out this week, with Seth and Mills in Paris and everything."

Suddenly, the world seems a lot brighter. "Cool," I say. I don't know Bailey all that well yet — he's quiet and keeps to himself — but Seth and he have really hit it off. And anything's better than having lunch on my own all week. Plus, he's not exactly hard on the eyes either.

We walk toward the playing fields and sit on the steps leading down to the hockey pitch. I'm chattering on about how Mr. Olen freaked out when Patrick shaved his head in class, claiming it was "performance art." Bailey doesn't say much, and after a while, I run out of things to talk about. We sit in silence for a moment, and I stare down at the hockey pitch while Bailey starts playing with the headphones hanging around his neck.

"You can put them on if you like," I say. "I don't mind. I know you need your regular music fix!"

"You sure?"

I nod. "'Course." I pull out my phone. "Need to work on my Beach Volleyball score, anyway."

He grins. "Cool." And pulling on his headphones, he begins bobbing his head to a track that sounds familiar. When it's finished, he takes them off.

"What were you listening to?" I ask.

"The Golden Lions. New Dublin band."

I practically leap off the step. "No way! The lead singer, Brains, is my Aunt Clover's boyfriend. But they haven't released anything yet. How did you—"

"Downloaded some tunes from their website. Tell Brains he's got a killer voice. Very distinctive."

We chat about music for a while, and then I say, "You know, I think Brains went to the same school as you: Lakelands. He's eighteen; he left last year. Do you remember him?"

He shakes his head. "Nah. I was only there for two terms."

"Why?" It's out before I can stop myself.

He winces and stares down at his headphones. (Sometimes I just can't leave well alone. I'm like a child with a scab on her knee—pick, pick, pick.)

"Sorry, I didn't mean to annoy you—" I begin.

"It's not a biggie. I didn't like Lakelands, so I left, end of story." He stands up. "Better motor. Books to sort—you know how it is. I'll see you around." And with that, he walks back toward the school, leaving me staring after him. What did I say?

I hear a titter to my right and look over: Sophie and the D4s. They must have followed us out. They're clearly not tired of tormenting me yet. Worse luck.

"Even the new boy doesn't want to hang with you, Green," Sophie sneers at me. "You're such a loser."

"Loser, loser, loser," all the D4s start to chant, like it's one of their stupid All Saints cheers.

I stand up and walk away quickly. One of them throws something at my back, but I don't turn around; I just keep walking.

As soon as I get in the door from school later that afternoon, Mum starts having a go at me. I'm *so* not in the mood.

"Much homework, Amy?" she asks, following me into the kitchen.

"A bit. I'll do it later."

She stands with her legs apart, puts her hands on her hips, and cocks her head, like a farmer about to round up her flock. All she's missing are the green wellies and the sheepdog. "You need to start as you mean to go on, Amy. Get cracking on it straightaway."

"But I'm hungry," I protest. "I can't study if my tummy's rumbling."

"I'll bring you up a sandwich."

"But you hate food upstairs. You say it encourages mice." I shudder at the thought. (We had a mouse once — in the airing cupboard. Dave found some droppings. Completely and utterly gross.) "Can I just hang out in the kitchen for a few minutes?" I beg. "Please? I've only just gotten in the door."

Mum softens a little. "I want you sitting at your desk in fifteen minutes, young lady. And mobile, please. Hand it over." She puts out her palm. "You can have it back once you're finished."

I stare at her. "You have got to be kidding me."

"I know you think second year will be a doddle — I've heard you talking to Mills and Clover about it — but it lays the foundation for your Junior Cert. exams."

Not again! "The exams are in *two* years, Mum. Get a grip."

She raises her eyebrows. "Do you want to end up stacking shelves or flipping burgers at McDonald's? Is that it?"

"There's nothing wrong with Macky D's. Stop being such a snob. Not everyone's cut out for college."

"Are you telling me you don't want to go to college? What are you going to do, then, eh?"

Oh, dear Lord, I'm so not interested in getting into this conversation now. I'm thirteen, for heaven's sake. How am I supposed to know what I want to do when I'm a wrinkly? Right now, I'm having enough trouble coping with school *sans* Mills and Seth. And what on earth has gotten into Mum? She's not usually such a nag.

"Can we have this conversation another time? As you pointed out, I have homework to do. A *lot* of homework. And I'd like to get on with it, if you don't mind. And for your information, I do want to go to college. At least, I think I do. But that's light-years away."

"It'll be on you quicker than you think." She pauses and brushes her hair back off her flushed face. "Then you'll have kids and be stuck at home with them all day, wasting your degree and wishing you'd had the good sense to be born a man."

OK, I get it. She's having one of her "I'm nearly forty and what have I got to show for it?" wobbles.

"Mum, once your new job starts, you won't be stuck at home with the babies all day," I say, softening my tone a little. "And you're still kind of young."

Her back stiffens. "I'm not talking about *me*, Amy. I'm talking generally."

Yeah, right.

"Can I please get something to eat now so I can hurry up and get on with my oh-so-important homework! Then I'll get all my exams and won't end up flipping burgers," I say in a rush.

"Fine," she says sniffily. "But I'll be up to check on your homework soon. No slacking off, understand?"

An hour later, I'm still sitting at my desk, staring into space. Luckily, Mum hasn't been near me — she's been too busy chasing after Alex and trying to stop Evie from crying (she's teething again) to bother.

I still haven't done my classics essay from Friday. I told Miss Sketchberry that I'd had to mind my baby bro and sis over the weekend — which is stretching the truth a little, I know. She looked a bit dubious but said she'd give me the benefit of the doubt. "But I want it tomorrow, understand? No excuses."

I also have geography (rivers), math (algebra), and history (the Renaissance) to do. Yawnsville. I mean, really — I get the Renaissance, and math is useful, but who needs to know the characteristics of a mature river? OK, apart from geography teachers. Pushing my books to one side, I pick up *Twilight* and start reading. And Mum picks that very moment to walk in the door. "Amy! What are you doing? You're supposed to be studying."

"It's our new class novel," I say.

She narrows her eyes. "I thought *To Kill a Mockingbird* was your class novel."

"That was last year."

"Hmmm." Mum doesn't seem convinced. Probably because I'm such a terrible liar.

"Can I use the computer?" I ask, trying to change the subject.

"Have you finished your homework?"

"Nearly."

"Show me."

Oops, scuppered. I'm saved by a yell from the hallway.

"Ma-ma, ma-ma." It's Alex. Bless him.

"I'll be back," Mum warns.

She's clearly out to torment me tonight, so I get stuck in immediately. No point jeopardizing my whole evening—Mills or Seth may have sent me a message.

I fly through the math, nail the classics essay and the history, and struggle through the geography. Forty-eight minutes later, it's all finito. I find Mum in the bathroom, washing Alex's teeth with his favorite purple cat toothbrush. Her hand is covered in spat-out toothpaste. I wince. Yuck! Remind me never to have kids.

"Can I use the computer now?" I say.

"Homework?"

"All on the desk and ready for inspection, sir." I click my heels together and salute.

Mum smiles. Her mood is obviously softening. "Good woman. And yes, you can use the computer. After dinner. Dave will be home in a minute and I'd like us all to eat together for once."

"Mum!"

"Go and set the table, Amy, and stop complaining."

Dinner is painful. Dave's so tired he almost falls asleep in his chicken curry, and Mum's not impressed.

"I go to all this trouble to cook, Dave," she moans, "and you can't even keep your eyes open. It's so unfair. Evie's been teething all day, and I've been slaving away in the house, dealing with Alex . . ."

Not again! I zone out and think about Seth and Mills. I wonder where they are right now. Probably sitting outside a fabulously cool Parisian café, shooting the breeze and eating—what do they eat in France? Snails, frogs' legs. Grim! OK, crêpes, they're yum!—crêpes with lots of chocolate sauce and ice cream and—

"Amy, your mum just asked what you're up to next weekend."

I sit up a little straighter. Dave is staring at me intently.

OK, I have to be careful here. I don't want to let the Parisian cat out of the bag. "It's my weekend to stay at Dad's, but with Gracie and everything, that's probably not going to happen."

"Maybe you can help me with the babies on Saturday," Dave suggests, looking at me pointedly. "We could take them to Cabinteely Park or something. Give your mum a bit of a break."

"Sure." I smile at him, safe in the knowledge that I won't be in the country.

Mum visibly relaxes, sinking down in her seat. A second later, her back goes rigid again. "You always say that, Dave, but it never happens. You slope off to write your stupid Dinoduck songs, and I end up with the babies again."

"No, honestly, Sylvie—this weekend will be different, I promise." He gives me a tiny wink.

"No kidding," I murmur.

"What was that, Amy?" Mum rounds on me.

"Nothing, Mum. Can I use the computer now?"

"Oh, for God's sake. Yes, fine! Use the bloomin' computer. And thank you so much for the lovely dinner, Mother, and for washing up and ironing my clothes. Oh, and for making sure there's enough food in the fridge and buying those ruddy Rice Krispie bars I seem to live on and—"

Dave puts his hand on Mum's arm. "Take it easy, Sylvie."

She shakes it off and continues her rant: "You're no better. I spend hours cooking a curry from scratch, toasting the spices, zesting limes, cutting up raw chicken with a knife—and you know how I hate that! You promised to sharpen my kitchen scissors, but you haven't bothered your barney yet, have you? And not even a lousy thank-you."

Dave squirms. "Give me a chance. It's delicious, Sylvie. Thank you. But next time, just order takeaway from Bombay Pantry if you're tired."

Mum looks disgusted. "Takeaway? Is my cooking that bad?"

Dave winces. "You're twisting my words, Sylvie. I just said . . ."

OK, I've had enough. Mum isn't being rational and this could go on for hours.

I stand up and put my plate and cutlery in the dishwasher. (No point enraging her further by forgetting.) I only hope to God she's cooled down by Friday—Paris will be zero fun with Mum in this kind of snit.

"Thank you for dinner, Mum," I say quietly, and slip out the door.

She's still taking lumps out of Dave, so I don't think she even notices.

In the living room, I click on the computer and

check my Facebook page. There's a new post from Mills: J'AIME PARIS. VIEW FROM THE ROOF OF THE SACRÉ CŒUR IS TO DIE FOR.

I smile to myself. Then I spot two new personal messages.

One is from Seth:

Hey, Amy,

Missing you so much, babes.

We arrived this morning. My host family is OK — quiet, though. Yves is 13 and doesn't say much. I think he's a bit of a sci-fi nerd — his room's full of *Star Trek* posters.

We went to an old church on top of a hill this afternoon — bit boring but stellar view. Annabelle refused to walk up all the steps — claimed she had a heart condition. Insisted on taking this ski lift thing while everyone else walked. Stupid wagon.

Hope Polly's OK. I told her to ring you if she needs anything. Hope that's cool with you.

More tomorrow.

Seth XXX

P.S. Glad you liked the heart. Cost me a fortune in popcorn.

Hey, Seth, I reply.

I don't tell him Bailey walked off — too embarrassing

Glad your host family is nice. School is dead without you and Mills. Hung out with Bailey at lunch, but that's about it. No news. My life is boring, boring, boring. And my mum's gone crazy mad, yet again.

Speaking of mums, 'course. Happy to help Polly — tell her to ring me anytime.

And please tell me all about Paris — I want to hear everything. What are the buildings like? Is it sunny? EVERYTHING.

Amy XXX

P.S. *J'ai beaucoup aimé* the heart!!! (Hope my French is right — I googled it.)

The other message is from Mills:

Dear Ames,

I'm here — in Paris! It's such a fab place. Plus, it's super sunny. Forgot my sunglasses — boo! Bought cool new ones — yeah!

My host family is really nice. Anais and Eriq Barnard are twins, 14 — both of them, obviously!

And Eriq is *fine*. Black hair, olive skin, sexy smile. Think Edward's face twinned with Jacob's tan and bod. Best of both *Twi*-worlds. Holy Moly! I know I got burned by the whole long-distance thing with Ed, but I may not be able to help myself!

Madame Barnard is a great cook—I'll be the size of an elephant when I get home—and their place is amazing! It's this cool apartment right in the middle of Montmartre, beside the Sacré Cœur—the church we visited earlier today with Miss Lupin. Lots of steps, but stunning view from the top.

How's Bailey? Tell him I was asking after him. Or maybe I should play it really cool. What do you think? Ho, hum, I don't know. You decide.

Anyway, have to mosey. I'm off to a café now with Eriq. He invited me to meet some of his friends—isn't that sweet?

À demain (that's "until tomorrow" in French!),
Mills XXXXXXXXXXXXX
P.S. Can't wait till Friday! I'm all set to implement Operation Seth—just give me the nod.

I sit back in my chair and before I know what's happening, tears are rolling down my cheeks. I miss

Seth and Mills so much, and it sounds like they're having so much fun without me. I know I'll be joining them on Friday, but how on earth am I going to cope with school until then?

Sophie and the D4s are only getting started. They're bound to torment me all week. Without Seth and Mills, I'm a sitting duck. Like I said, Sophie, Mills, and I used to be friends, and I know a lot about Sophie — probably too much. The D4s are ultra competitive about everything, including coming from a perfect 2.4 family. Annabelle's always bringing in newspaper clippings of her dad and "famous" mum looking like the perfect couple at charity events and balls. Barf. (Annabelle's mum was an "Irish model" before she got hitched, which basically means she was too short or too curvy to be a catwalk model, so she just appeared in a bikini selling cars instead.)

Sophie's less-than-ideal background is the chink in her armor, so she tells everyone her dad has a big-shot job at an oil company in Bahrain and doesn't get home very often. (I bet half of them don't even know where Bahrain is.) But I know the truth. Like I said, Sophie rarely sees him now he lives in London with his second family. The fact that I know her secret is partly why she hates me so much.

I guess I'll just have to keep out of her way this

week. I'd pull a sickie, but staying at home with Mum in one of her moods would be just as bad. No, I'll just have to get on with it. And I'm sure Bailey will have come around by tomorrow, even if I did accidentally annoy him by mentioning his old school.

With a sigh, I brush away my tears and reply to Mills, trying to sound cheerier than I feel.

♥ Chapter 17

By Tuesday evening, I'm fairly convinced that Bailey really is avoiding me. He sat at the back during English class (slid in beside Sophie Piggott, of all people) instead of in his usual place. Sophie was thrilled and spent most of the class trying to chat him up, much to Miss Bingley's annoyance. "This isn't a speed-dating event, Sophie," she said dryly. "Please stop batting your eyelids at Mr. Otis."

At lunch break, I looked for him at the science block, but he wasn't there. It was sunny for the second day in a row and really warm — an Indian summer, my gran would have called it — so most people were sitting outside. I had two choices: hang by myself, like Billy-no-mates, or join the D4s. Ha! As if.

I came up with a third option — skip eating lunch and read *Twilight* on the closed loo seat in the top loos, hoping that no one would wonder why the cubicle was occupied for so long. Sad, I know, but it was nice and quiet, and at least in there the D4s couldn't flick their food at me (which happened at little break — and let me tell you, grated cheese is a killer to get out of your hair) or call me names. Today they moved on from "loser" to "raisin face." Not exactly original, but equally hurtful. I walked around with my hand cupped over my chin all day, trying to hide the new outcrop of spots, but I think it just drew more attention to them, not less.

With a sigh, I check my phone again. Dad still hasn't replied to my message. I texted him on the DART on the way home, reminding him that he promised I could visit Gracie tomorrow afternoon and suggesting he meet me at Connolly DART station so we could walk up to the hospital together, just the two of us. I'm really psyched about it. It's been ages since I've had Dad to myself, and I can't wait to tell him all about the Paris trip, and see Gracie again, of course. I wonder if she's changed — babies grow pretty quickly.

I can't believe Dad hasn't gotten back to me yet. I throw my mobile down on the bed beside me. At least Mum forgot to confiscate it today. She's still in mega bully-Amy-into-studying mode, though. "No computer privileges until your work is done, young lady," she said the minute I walked through the front door.

Privileges? What planet is she on? Planet Homework Nazi?

Thankfully, once I get started, it doesn't take long to plow through my homework: Spanish (groan), Irish (double groan), and science. I lay it all out for Mum's approval. Once she's given me the OK, I skip downstairs. Logging on to Facebook has become the highlight of my day. How pitiful is that?

There's a brief "missing you loads" PM from Seth and another longer e-mail from Mills:

Dear Amy,

I SO wish you were here. I urgently need your advice, O wise one.

That café Eriq took me to last night was amazing, and his friends are so cool, real music heads like Bailey. Although, they have very dodgy taste — weird French rap. And it's not just a language thing, the music's *très* odd too. Then Eriq and I walked home together and he kissed me on the doorstep!

And oh, Amy, it's true, all that stuff about French boys. His kissing was out of this world! My knees went all weak and I lurched against him, nearly taking him down too — soooo embarrassing, but he thought it was funny.

He was really sweet to me at breakfast — made me hot chocolate in a bowl. (That must be a French thing, or else they'd run out of clean mugs.) Then we walked to school together, and that's when the trouble started.

After a whole morning of French classes (as thrilling as it sounds, not!), we climbed the Eiffel Tower with the French students, and everything was going great. Eriq took my hand going up the steps (which took ages — there are oodles of them). On the viewing platform at the top we bumped into Annabelle, who had insisted on taking the lift. She went into fits of laughter when she saw we were holding hands. Eriq asked her why she was laughing, and she said, in front of everyone, that back in Dublin I was deeply uncool and the biggest loser in the whole of Saint John's!

Then she started telling him about that time in first year when I came into school dressed up as Cleopatra for classics, only I got the day wrong, so I was the only one in costume, you remember?

"So what?" I told her. "It was an honest mistake, and Miss Sketchberry said I made a very good Cleopatra."

She made a face at me then and launched into another story — about that time I fell into the duck pond on the open farm trip and stank of pondweed all the way home. Then she only opened her mouth about me wetting my pants in Junior Infants. But I was five, Amy, FIVE! It's so unfair. She made it sound like it happened recently. At that stage, Eriq looked at me, his eyes all cold, dropped my hand, and walked off, in front of everyone! I was left standing there on my own like a lemon, with Annabelle sniggering away. I've never been so embarrassed in my whole entire life! Now Eriq's treating me like I have some sort of infectious disease.

And the worst thing is: I can't stop thinking about him! But now that I'm a Parisian social pariah, he'll never like me.

What should I do? I really, really want him to like me again, Amy!

Help!!!

Mills XXXXXXXXXXXXX

I bristle. That's just great. I know I should feel outrage at what Annabelle did and sympathy for Mills — even if Eriq does sound like a prize eejit — but she's so caught up in her own Parisian problems she hasn't even stopped to ask how things are back in Dublin and how *I'm* feeling. I'm just about to e-mail her back, to say how lousy things are in Dublin too and to tell her that she's not the only one feeling fed up, when there's a loud *BEEP:* a text message on my mobile. It's from Dad: SORRY, AMY, TOMORROW MAY NOT SUIT — HAVE TO DRIVE PAULINE TO DUNDRUM SC. SHE CLAIMS IT'S URGENT. SHELLY NEEDS CUSHIONS FOR THE NURSERY OR SOMETHING. IS SAT OK? DAD X

Siúcra. No, Saturday's not OK. I'll be in France on Saturday. I need to talk to him in person. It's all too complicated for a text message.

I type back: CAN I RING U?

BETTER NOT. IN HOSPITAL WITH SHELLY, AND DOCTOR DUE ANY MIN. TALK ON SAT.

Oh, this is just getting better and better. First Mills, now my Dad. Does anyone have time for *me*? *I'm not going to be here on Saturday, you stupid man,* I want to scream. *That's what I'm trying to talk to you about!*

I sit back against my pillow grumpily and stare down at my phone in frustration. Dad doesn't have time for me these days, and Mills and Seth are no use to me this week. I have no one to talk to. No one. Then it dawns on me: Clover always has time for me. I ring her.

"Hey, Bean Machine," she says breezily. "Can I ring you back later? I'm in the middle of writing something and I need to get it finished."

"Fine," I snap, clicking off the phone.

Some days are just so rubbish.

♥ Chapter 18

Wednesday means a half day and no lunch break, hurrah! I skip extra hockey practice — it's fitness, and come on, how fit does a goalie need to be? Our forwards are so good that most of the match is played in the other team's circle, anyway, and I spend a lot of the time hitting small stones off the Astroturf with my hockey stick or daydreaming about Seth.

It's suspiciously quiet when I get home. I check the kitchen and the garden: no sign of Mum or the babies. I'm pleased. A bit of peace will make up for the fact that I would be visiting Gracie right about now were it not for my useless dad. I flop down on the sofa in the living room and flick on the telly. Time to catch up with the shows I've saved on the Sky box before Dave deletes them to make room for

Top Gear. Every birthday and Christmas I buy him the DVDs, but he still insists on taping the blooming things. (There should be a law against *Top Gear* if you ask me.)

Just then my mobile rings.

"Amy?"

"Hi, Mum."

"What's all the noise?"

I quickly press MUTE. "Just the radio." (Mum hates me watching telly in the afternoon. Says it's a one-way ticket to the dole queues. How she's figured that one out I really don't know.)

"No telly till your homework's done, OK?"

I ignore her. "Where are you?"

"At Monique's with Evie. Gramps took Alex off my hands, bless him. They're going on the train. As it's free for old-age pensioners, Gramps says he'll read his paper and travel from Howth to Bray and back again until they both get hungry."

I laugh. "Great idea." Alex would spend all day every day on a bus or train if he could. "What time are you back, Mum?"

"Sixish. I'll get some fish and chips on the way home. I can't be bothered to cook."

"Cool." I try not to sound too excited. This is all most excellent news indeed.

"You OK?" she asks. "You sound a bit funny."

"I'm fine—honest," I say, trying to keep the bubbles of joy under control. "See you later." I click off my mobile and sink back into the sofa.

It's only half two. More than three hours of peace and Sky box. Bliss! Watching telly means I don't have to think about Mills or Dad or Clover and how useless they all are. Plus, only one more lunch break to endure before Paris.

Things are finally looking up.

I'm in my room later that evening when my mobile rings. It's Clover. "Hey, Beanie. Anything up? Sorry I couldn't talk yesterday, but Saffy was breathing down my neck. I was late with my piece on love potions and spells for the Halloween issue. I found this white witch in Wicklow called Olywena and got her to write it for me. Said she'd do it if she could plug her new book at the end. But her spelling and grammar were appalling. I practically had to rewrite the whole darn thing. Took me ages."

"Hey, Clover," I say, smiling to myself. (Only Clover could find a white witch in Wicklow willing to do her dirty work for her.) My anger melts away. I guess she can't always be there for me when I need her.

I must still sound a bit peeved with her, though, because she says, "You sound a bit glum-dum-dum. You OK, babes?"

"Not really. I had another rubbish day in school." As I tell her what's been happening since Monday, a lump starts forming in my throat. I gulp it back. "With Mills and Seth both away, I have no one to talk to, and the D4s have decided it's pick-on-Amy week. I feel like such a reject. Even Dad's too busy to see me—he canceled today's visit. Took Pauline shopping instead. Shelly needs cushions for the nursery, apparently."

She tut-tuts. "Sorry to hear that, but I'm afraid your dad's a bit of a marshmallow when it comes to what Shelly-darling wants. And once Seth and Mills are back, I'm sure the D4s will find another target for their evilness. You're nearly there—only one more day, Beanie. Besides, being alone isn't always such a horrible thing. You have to learn to be cool with it—it's an acquired skill. There's a big difference between being alone and being lonely."

She clicks her tongue and then goes on, her voice a little flat: "Brains is working his little tush off these days and I barely get to see him, but I've had to learn to deal with it. Sometimes I throw myself into work, or read, or watch telly, or check Facebook, or chat to you. And you know what really keeps my mind off it? Helping other people. I get a real kick out of answering the problem-page letters and giving readers a leg up. Even though I spend a lot of time in my office, alone, I've chosen not to be lonely. Do you get what I'm saying?"

"I think so." I sigh — a big, hopeless, raggedy sigh.

"No one said being a teen was easy, my friend," Clover says. "But whoa, horsey, enough of this serious stuff. You looking forward to Paris on Friday, babes?"

"Can't wait."

"How are Mills and Seth getting on?"

"Seth's fine but Mills is having a small *garçon* problem. What's new? She's staying with a host family and she snogged the son, Eriq."

Clover giggles. "Way to go, Mills! Guess she's over Ed, then."

"Guess so. But Annabelle Hamilton told him some stories about Mills — embarrassing stuff, like the time she wet her knickers in Junior Infants — and now he won't speak to her."

Clover gasps. "No! That Hamilton girl's nasty, nasty. And the French-fry guy doesn't sound much better. Tell Auntie Clover everything. And I mean every juicy little morsel. Methinks Mills is looking for advice, am I right?"

"Yep. I don't know all that much, but I'll tell you what I do know. . . ."

When I've finished telling her all about Mills and Eriq, she launches into loads of fab suggestions as to how Mills can fix things. I smile again. Clover's right: helping people does make you feel better.

"Hey, Beanie," Clover concludes, "this would make a great *Goss* problem-page letter. Can we publish it if the names are changed?"

I nod. "I'm sure Mills wouldn't mind if we protect her identity. We gave her advice on how to make Ed notice her in the *Goss*, remember? And she loved that."

"Awesome." Clover layers on her best Noo Yawk accent. (She's amazing at accents.) "Let's give her a kickin' reply to her man woes. The agony aunt dream team is back in action, so help me, *Gawd*."

And this is what we came up with:

Dear Paris,

    The guy you've described sounds like a real skank monkey. Turning against you on the word of just one girl. For all he knows, she's lying to get into his *pantalons*. Humiliating stories shouldn't be regurgitated like that — it's just not cricket. But we all have embarrassing tales to tell, believe me. No one's past is squeaky-clean. So hold your head up high, girl. You have nothing to be ashamed of.

First things first: are you sure you want this boy-creature from the black lagoon back in your life, girlfriend? Supa sure? If so, we think we can help. You want to make him fall head over heels for you again? Then here's the plan:

❤ **Spice up your image.**
Show him how fab and original you really are, and prove dumbo-girl wrong. Demonstrate your cool credentials. Add a sprinkle of pizzazz, a dollop of glama. Be original — how about a hat and some killer biker boots teamed with shorts and sparkly tights? If you look cool, you'll feel confident and sassy.

❤ **Pretend to forget his name, or get him mixed up with someone else.**

Act as if you couldn't care less about him. Surround yourself with friends, and smile and laugh, especially if he's near. Pretend you don't give a hoot, and back he'll shoot.

🖤 Ignore him completely!

Nothing makes a boy's blood boil more than the silent treatment. If he confronts you, say, "Little old *moi*? I'm not ignoring you; I just don't have anything to say to you. You believe that girl over me, you must be stupid, and I don't like guys with straw for brains." Ouch! Gotta hurt!

🖤 Flirt with another boy.

For safety's sake, pick a friend or someone you know won't take it too seriously. What you don't need is even more boy trouble, my friend.

Do all this and he'll soon realize he can't live without you! But here's the thing—maybe when he does come crawling back, you'll realize you *can* live without him. Think about it! Life's too short to date a creep unless he's honestly, truly changed.

Good luck!

Love and bubbles,

Clover and Amy XXX

After I put down the phone to Clover, I'm in a much better humor. I go downstairs and check my Facebook messages. Nothing from Mills, but this from Seth:

The *Mona Lisa*

For Amy

I'm staring at the *Mona Lisa*,
But all I can think of is you.
The way your eyes shine when you laugh,
The way your nose crinkles when you're angry,
The way you kiss your fingers and blow them
    at me,
At me.
And the way you look at me, really look at me,
As if I'm the center of your world.
The way you smile,
A smile to light up the universe,

To set a body free.
How can I admire the *Mona Lisa*'s smile,
When yours is the one that truly matters?

Can't wait to see you Monday. Everything's black-and-white without you.
Love,
Seth X

I read the poem again. It's not exactly Seamus Heaney but it's heartfelt and it makes me smile. It's the second poem Seth's written for me — the first one was last summer, when he was in Italy and I was in West Cork. I print it out for my diary and then hug the paper against my chest.

♥ Chapter 19

On Thursday evening, my mobile rings. "Amy, are you in your room?" It's Dad and for some reason he's whispering.

"Yes, why?" I'm sorting through my clothes for Paris and keeping out of Mum's way. (Dave's working extra hours again this evening and she's not happy about it.)

"Where's your mum?"

"Bathing the babies." I can hear the shrieks and splashes through my door.

"Good. Think you can sneak outside? And don't let your mum see you, understand?"

"Outside? Dad, what's going on?"

"Shush, keep it down — she'll hear you. I'm parked opposite the Starrs' place. Hurry!" He hangs up.

OK, none of this is making any sense. Dad's behaving very strangely, but I'm intrigued.

I sneak out of my room, past the bathroom, down the stairs, and out the front door, closing it quietly behind me. Outside, it takes me a second to spot him. His car's parked behind a van and he's slumped down in his seat. I head toward him.

"Hi, Dad," I say, pulling open the passenger door.

He jumps and clutches his chest. "Amy!"

I climb in and stare at him. "Are you all right? You're acting really weird."

He sighs. "Your mother's hopping mad with me and I don't fancy being shouted at again, so I'm trying to keep a low profile."

"Why? What have you done now?"

"She's annoyed that I blew off your hospital visit yesterday to go shopping."

"Ah, that." He's right; Mum was less than impressed. She used some pretty strong language when I told her.

"I don't know why I even bothered going. Guess what happened." He continues without pausing for me to answer. "As soon as we got to Dundrum Pauline dumped me! Sat me down in Butlers Chocolate Café and told me to wait. Said I'd only get in the way.

Three flaming hours I was sitting in that café on my own, like an eejit. I ate so many chocolates it'll take me weeks in the gym to burn the calories off."

"Shouldn't have eaten them all, then, should you?" I say, smiling. Leaving Dad in a chocolate café is like leaving Alex in a toy shop.

"I was bored, Amy. I couldn't help myself. Now and again she'd come back to drop bags off, but apart from that I was on my tod. Read the *Irish Times* from cover to cover, even the letters page and all the small ads." He sniffs. "Pauline bought loads of cushions for Gracie's room, pink flowery things. And she never even asked if I liked them."

"And did you?"

He shrugs. "Amy, men aren't interested in cushions. I couldn't care less what Gracie sits on as long as she's healthy. I just wanted to be asked. To feel involved, needed, you know? It's the principle of the thing. I had driven her all the way down there!" I stare at him. It's not like Dad to be such a wuss. "And then when we got back, Shelly pretty much ignored me at dinner," he goes on. "Spent the whole time discussing color schemes for Gracie's room with her mum. Pauline doesn't like the yellow, says it doesn't complement Gracie's skin tone and that pink or coral would be more suitable."

I try not to yawn but fail miserably.

"Sorry, Amy. I know I'm probably boring you rigid, but I don't have anyone else to talk to." He stops for a moment. "Anyway, enough about me. How are you? School OK?"

"Fine," I say with a shrug. I don't want to talk about it. This week has crawled by like a camel on its knees. Getting picked on every day isn't exactly my idea of fun.

After a few seconds' silence, Dad continues, "Look, I am sorry about yesterday." He runs his hands through his hair, leaving wide finger ridges. "I hadn't realized you'd be away this weekend until Dave rang and told me about the surprise trip. He had a bit of a go at me about the whole hospital thing too. If I'd known you were so bothered about seeing Gracie, I would have arranged another visit, honest. Why didn't you say something about Paris?"

"I didn't get the chance: you texted and asked me not to ring you, remember? You haven't exactly been Mr. Contactable."

Silence. Dad stares out of the windscreen. "Sorry," he says eventually. "Are you annoyed with me too, Amy?"

What am I supposed to say? Yes, I'm completely fed up. School is rubbish and you're acting like I don't exist. Gracie is my sister, my *sister*; I'm worried about her and I have a right to see her. But it sounds self-absorbed, and Dad's already been getting it in the neck from Mum and Dave. He hardly needs anymore aggro from me. Plus, if I give out to him too much, who knows . . . ? Maybe our relationship will become like Sophie and her dad's, and I couldn't bear that. No, it's best not to rock the boat.

"No, not really." I stare down at my hands and scratch at a hangnail.

Dad smiles gently. "I'm so glad you've inherited my calm nature, Amy. Sylvie can be such a hothead sometimes. You never cause a fuss, do you, eh?" He reaches over to ruffle my hair, but I pull my head away.

I know Mum can be a bit emotional, but at least you know exactly how she's feeling. With Dad, it's different. There's always this veneer, like a sheet of ice over his emotions. It's hard to make out what he's thinking half the time.

"Did I ever tell you about the time she threw her boots at me in Central Park?" he says.

I shake my head. I'm torn. Dad's being a bit disloyal—I don't think Mum would appreciate him telling me personal stories, especially ones about her losing it—but then again it does sound interesting.

"Her boots?" I ask.

Dad nods. "Her boots. We'd just had lunch at the Boathouse—where Carrie and Mr. Big used to meet, apparently."

My eyes light up. "Wow! What's it like?"

"I don't really remember. Nice views of the lake, though. I made sure we got the best table. Anyway, I had to take a couple of work calls during lunch and she wasn't impressed. Didn't say a word to me until we got outside the door, then she hunkered down, took off her boots, and threw them at my head."

"Why?"

He shrugs. "Nothing major. I promised I'd turn off my BlackBerry during lunch, but there was this deal going through. It only rang a couple of times, but your mum seemed to take offense. Even though I took them all outside."

"How many times, exactly?"

"I don't know, seven, eight?"

"Dad!"

He puts his hands up. "Hey! Someone has to bring in the money. No deals, no moolah. That's life, Amy."

I think of Mum sitting all alone at a restaurant table in New York, waiting for Dad to get off the phone. Poor Mum. *It was only one deal, Dad,* I want to tell him. *And you broke a promise.* But I keep my mouth shut.

"Anyway, how's Gracie?" I say instead. "You haven't mentioned her yet."

Dad hits his forehead with his hand. "What *am* I thinking? She's doing great. The hole's closed over and they're just monitoring her now to check there are no further complications."

"That's brilliant, Dad. I can't wait to see her again."

"I know, love." He puts his hand over mine, at the same time as glancing at his watch. "Listen, I'd better get home. Shelly will be wondering where I've gotten to, and I'm sure Pauline will have a list of things for me to do."

"Shelly's home?"

"Of course. Picked her up on the way back from Dundrum yesterday after the doctor had done a final checkup. Didn't I say?"

"No."

"Sorry. I'm very forgetful at the moment." He leans over and pecks me on the cheek. "Enjoy Paris. Your mum and I were there — gosh, it must be more than twelve years ago now. Second honeymoon. Very romantic." He gives me a wink and starts up the engine.

"Dad!"

He just grins. "See you when you get back."

The minute I've climbed out and shut the door behind me, he's driving away. I watch the car for a second before it disappears around the corner, then I begin walking back toward the house.

As I'm crunching up the drive, something occurs to me. Last autumn, when I went on a hockey trip to Wales, he arrived the night before with a bag of sterling coins for the slot machines, plus twenty pounds spending money. This time he didn't give me so much as one yo-yo to spend in Paris, and we use the same currency. I'm trying not to be mercenary about it, but even a fiver would have done.

I push open the front door, hoping to sneak back upstairs without being spotted but . . .

"There you are!" Dave pops out of the living room as soon as I walk inside, making me jump. (He must have just gotten back from work.)

I give a surprised shriek and he says, "Shush! Evie's in bed."

"You're the one who jumped out at me," I grumble. "Do you want something?"

He smiles. "Sorry—didn't mean to frighten you. Just wanted to catch you alone. I spotted you in the car with Art and thought I'd wait to talk to you. Why didn't he come in? Scared of Sylvie having a go at him, was he?"

I laugh. "Something like that."

"Now," Dave goes on, "I just wanted to tell you that once Sylvie's in bed, I'll put her suitcase in the cupboard under the stairs for the morning, OK?"

"Where is it now?"

"In the boot of my car. It's almost packed. I just have to find her shampoo and stuff. What else will she need in the way of toiletries? Shower gel, toothbrush, and toothpaste. Will that cover it?"

I shake my head. Boys really are clueless.

♥ Chapter 20

It seems like I've just gotten to sleep when I feel some-one shaking me, hard. "Wakey, wakey, sleepyhead." It's Clover.

"I can't. It's way too early. Please don't make me." I groan loudly and clamp my pillow over my head.

Ignoring my plea, Clover flicks on my bedroom light and peels the pillow back. "What are you talking about, Beanie. It's three fifty. Monique will be here in ten minutes, like we arranged. We all have to surprise Sylvie together, remember?"

"Ten minutes?" I wail. "I'll never be ready in ten minutes!" (I haven't even finished packing. *Siúcra!*)

I roll over and push myself up. My head throbs and my eyes feel all dry and itchy. I rub them with a knuckle and yawn so deeply my jaw almost dislocates.

Clover's just standing there, smiling. "You're such a lazybones."

"Why are you grinning at me like a mentaller?" I moan. "It's too early to be happy."

"I'm hyperexcited. Paris, Beanie. *Paris!*" She hugs herself.

"But you hate mornings too."

"It's not morning to me, 'cos I haven't actually been to sleep. Clever, eh? I pumped myself full of Gramps's tar-thick espresso last night. Seven cups. I'm still buzzing."

I squint at her. "Are you sure you're in a fit state to drive?"

"*Perfecto.* Made it this far, didn't I? The rest's mainly motorway."

Now that my eyes have finally focused, I can see that hers are darting around the room and she's jiggling up and down like a toddler on a bouncy castle. An *über*hyper Clover: just what I need when I'm feeling like a giant sloth.

"Throw your clothes on, Beanie. Chop, chop."

"Would you mind giving me some privacy?" I say, a little primly. "Turn around."

"Ooooooh, *privacy*," she teases. "Nothing I haven't seen before. I used to change your nappy, remember?"

"When you were five, Clover? Really?"

"Well, maybe not. Still, no need to be shy, Bean Machine."

I glare at her and she says, "OK, OK. I get the message. You're *so* not a morning lark. I'll wait outside."

As soon as she's gone, I shudder into action. I grab the pile of clothes I sorted last night and throw it into my travel bag. There's no time to think about coordination: I'll just have to make do with what I have and hope Clover will let me borrow some of her clothes. She's bound to have overpacked. Next I zip up my makeup bag and wrap it in a hoodie like Clover taught me, so it won't get smashed by the baggage handlers.

I'm just doing up my case when Clover pops her head around the door again. "Beanie!" She scowls. "You're still in your pajamas."

"I thought I'd wear them on the plane: nice and comfy."

She looks at me as if I'm mad.

I roll my eyes. "I'm joking."

"Good. Monique just texted me. ETA: three minutes."

"Get out and I'll be ready in two seconds."

"You'd better be," Clover warns, shutting the door. "Otherwise, I am bundling you into the car in your PJs. We're tight on time as it is."

I grab the first clean things I can find and get dressed in record time.

When I open my bedroom door, Monique is standing in the hall beside Clover. She's wearing a floaty black-and-white-striped top over red skinny jeans and looks remarkably awake for this hour of the morning.

She grins at me. "Hi, Amy," she whispers. "Ready to surprise your mum?"

I nod and yawn again.

"Got your CD player?"

"Oops." I fetch it from my room and plug it in at Monique's feet.

Clover crouches down, slips a CD in, and presses PLAY. "All shipshape and ready to go, Captain Monny." She salutes her finger to her temple. "Link arms and let's rock this joint."

Monique throws one long arm around Clover's shoulder and the other around mine. As soon as the music starts playing — not too loudly: we don't want to wake the babies — I open Mum and Dave's bedroom door and we shuffle inside and stand at the foot of the bed.

"Now, girls!" Monique says, flicking on the light.

We start kicking our legs in the air and singing along to the French cancan music. Clover and I are giggling so much we can hardly keep up with Monique. "Da, da, da-da-da-da, da, da . . ."

Mum opens her eyes, shuts them tightly, and then opens them again. "Am I dreaming?" she says, pushing herself to a sitting position. "Girls, have you gone completely crazy? What's happening? Have I forgotten my own birthday?"

We stop dancing and Monique says, "Sylvie, you're off to Paris! Now. With us. Flight leaves in less than three hours."

Mum stares at her. "Paris? What are you on about?"

"Your bridesmaids are kidnapping you, Sylvie," Dave says with a monster grin. He's chuckling away to himself, enjoying Mum's confusion. "It's all arranged. Your bag's ready and waiting—it's in the cupboard under the stairs—and I've taken time off to mind the kids."

"I made sure he packed your makeup, your hair dryer, your special conditioner, and your frizzy-hair stuff, Mum," I add. "And some decent clothes."

Mum suddenly puts her hands over her face and starts sobbing loudly.

Clover pulls a face. "Yikes. Wasn't quite the reaction we were hoping for, Sylvie."

But when Mum peels her hands away, she's beaming through her tears. "This is the nicest thing anyone's ever done for me. Thank you. All of you." She throws her arms around Dave and gives him a big smacker on the lips.

"Remind me to arrange surprise trips more often," Dave says to us with a wink.

"You were in on this from the start?" Mum asks him.

He grins. "Pretty much. But it was Clover and Monique's idea."

She looks at me. "And you, Amy?"

"They only told me a couple of weeks ago," I admit. "They were worried I'd let the cat out of the bag."

"You?" Mum smiles. "Never."

"Ha, ha," I say, slightly miffed. "I can keep secrets, you know."

"'Course you can, Beanie," Clover says, then glances at her watch. "Eek! Better mush, Sylvie, or we'll miss the flight."

After another big smooch with Dave, Mum jumps out of bed. "Do I have time for a shower?"

"No!" we all yell.

"You'll just have to be smelly," Clover adds.

We're soon flying down the M50 on the way to Dublin Airport. Cramming all the bags into Clover's Mini Cooper was interesting, but Dave managed to get the boot shut somehow, and now Monique and I are squeezed into the backseat, our feet resting on the smaller travel bags.

The last thing Dave did before we drove off was to hand me the passports. I put them in the pink leather travel wallet Dad gave me the first time we flew transatlantic. I'm a bit paranoid about losing it, so I'm clutching it on my knee. I stroke the cool leather and think about Dad, wondering how Gracie is doing and imagining her lying in the hospital, pretty much oblivious to my existence. How can she know how much I love her when I've barely seen her? My eyes well up a little.

"OK, Amy?" Monique asks quietly.

I blink back my tears and nod.

"Did you remember your passport this time?" I ask Clover, to deflect attention from me.

Deathly silence.

"Clover, did you hear what I just said?"

"*Póg, póg*, and triple *póg*," Clover mutters. "I knew there was something." She looks down at the Mini's clock, and in the rearview mirror I can see she's nearly chewing her lip off.

"Ah, Clover, not again!" Mum groans. (With Clover and flying, there's always something. Last summer, we almost missed our connection from London to Miami 'cos she wanted to check out just about every shop at Heathrow's duty-free. She had to flirt with a guard so he'd swift track us through security. I think she's airport jinxed!)

"Don't panic," she says. "I'll ring Gramps and he can meet us halfway."

Mum tut-tuts. "Poor Dad. That's all he needs."

"Got any better ideas?" Clover asks tartly.

Monique jumps in quickly to prevent an argument. "Let's not fight, girls," she says. "It's only a minor blip. We'll still make it."

Clover rings Gramps, and luckily, he finds it amusing and agrees to do a mercy passport dash. He must have really pegged it, 'cos less than twenty minutes later, he pulls up behind us where we're illegally parked on the Ballymount overpass and steps out of his Volvo in his dressing gown and checked slippers. "A father's work is never done," he says with a twinkle in his eye as Clover buzzes down her window. "I believe you might be needing this, Miss Wildgust."

He hands her the passport through the window and slaps the roof of the Mini. "*Bon voyage,* ladies. Behave yourselves."

"As if," Clover says with a wicked grin.

♥ Chapter 21

In the end, our flight's delayed and we have plenty of time at the airport. After checking in our bags and going through security without a hitch, Mum and Monique mooch around the duty-free, spritzing themselves with expensive perfume.

"I'm off to find somewhere to crash," Clover says, after trailing them for a little while. "I'm feeling a leetle bit dizzy."

"Not surprised. You've missed a whole night's sleep, Clover." I wander around with her until she finds a block of seats near our departure gate to lie on. Within minutes, she's snoozing away, making funny snore-click noises at the back of her throat.

I sit down for a bit, but I forgot to pack my book, so I have nothing to read. I'm just wondering what to do when I spot a computer terminal. Aha!

I log in, hoping for something from Seth. (I'm itching to see him — not long now.) There's nothing from him, but there is a PM from Mills:

Dear Amy,

OMG, you and Clover are such geniuses! Thanks for e-mailing me those ideas. I put them into practice, and guess what! It worked! Eriq's all over me like a rash now — just can't get enough, as the old song goes.

After some judicious dressing — shorts, sparkly tights, Converse boots — some flirting with Milo, and ignoring him most of yesterday, Eriq is now paying me lots of attention, which is driving Annabelle wild. You were right: she does fancy him!

But here's the thing: now that he's following me around like a lapdog, I'm not all that sure I like him. I got an e-mail from Bailey yesterday, saying he missed me. Swoon!

Who should I choose? I don't know what to do. Help!

Your megaconfused friend,

Mills XXXXXXXXXXXXXXXXXXXXXXX

P.S. Is it all systems go for Operation Seth? Just give me my orders, Sergeant Green!

I sigh. Confused is right. I love her to bits, but sometimes she drives me completely bonkers. (And I have no idea what Milo will have made of her flirting with him — he probably thinks she's gone gaga.) I don't know why I bother trying to untwist her romantic tangles; she always seems to wade obliviously into yet more boy drama, mostly of her own creation, no matter what I say.

Well, missy, you're on your own this time. I've done my bit. It's time to sort out your own relationship doo-doo.

Dear Mills,

No idea what this means, but it sounds vague enough to cover most things.

Sorry to hear you're in a boy pickle again. I'm sure it will all come out in the wash.

Now, to Operation Seth. Make sure you put the discussed item in Seth's backpack this morning before you set out. Thanks, buddy!

See you in Paris!

Amy XXX

♥ 204

I only hope she's not too addled by her angel-faced *garçon* to concentrate on what really matters: surprising Seth. Only a few hours until our dastardly plan will be fully operational. I can't wait.

"There you are, Amy," Mum says as I'm logging out of Facebook. She walks toward me, Monique trailing behind her, slugging back a bottle of water. "Bought you some things for the flight," she adds, handing me a plastic bag.

I look inside: bottle of water, Polo mints, Tayto crisps, a Sarah Dessen book I've already read (but will happily read again), and the latest issue of the *Goss*.

"Thanks, Mum."

We rejoin Clover, who's still sleeping, and I settle down in the spare seat beside her and dig into my goodies. It's getting busier now, and Mum and Monique have to hunt around before they are able to find two seats together. They are by the window and next to a businessman in a dark suit. The two of them wave over at me and gesture at the man with their heads, giggling and nudging each other. I look at him — he's OK looking for an old, I guess, but please! They're behaving like idiots, so I just ignore them.

Pulling out the mag, I flick to the problem page first. It still gives me a thrill to see "Ask Clover and Amy: any problem solved!" printed at the top of the page.

Then I spot an article on the following page:

HOW TO MAKE A BOY FALL IN LOVE WITH YOU FROM SOMEONE WHO KNOWS — 'COS HE'S ONE TOO!

Here's some advice, girls:

1. **First up: always be yourself.**
   We can spot fakes a mile off.

2. **Smile!**
   Nothing cute about a grumpy chick. Wipe that sour look off your face. Warm and sunny, that's what's attractive.

3. **Stop using the telly and mags as your style bibles (yes, even the *Goss*).**
   And don't just follow the baa-baa-Uggly-boot sheep. We do like girls with their own original look — but actually boys care a lot less about clothes than you think. And don't wear shoes you can't walk in. FYI — we're sick and tired of carrying you home.

4. Be confident and sass-sass-sassy.

Nothing sexier than a girl who knows who she is and ain't afraid to show it.

5. Learn how to take a compliment.

When we tell you you're looking fine, just smile and say "thanks." Don't tell us we're blind/deranged — we might start believing it. And we certainly won't compliment you again.

6. Stop with the stage-school makeup.

We don't like being glued to your lips with industrial gloss; and we hate fake-tan marks on our favorite tees.

7. Take a hint!

If we're walking close, bumping shoulders with you, it means we'd like to hold your hand.

8. Boys are human too.

Don't play games. And if we've done something wrong, tell us. We're not mind readers.

9. Allow us to be big kids sometimes.

Snowball fights, silly jokes, Xbox, and just plain old thumping each other — boys will be boys!

10. Be kind and respect our feelings.

It takes a lot of courage for a guy to say, "I love you." Whatever you do, don't laugh. If you need more time, be honest and have the guts to admit it.

11. Give nice guys a break.

Not all lads are out to break your heart.

12. And finally — I'll say it again, 'cos it's ultra NB (*important-te*) — always be yourself. We like you for who you are, not what you are. Remember that.

"What are you reading, Beanie?" Clover says, sitting up and stretching. She leans over to see, then smiles. "Ah, thought it might interest you. Guess who wrote it."

"No idea."

She grins. "Brains, of course! He does work for the *Goss* when he's not gigging. Good, isn't it? I reckon the 'let boys be boys' bit is directed at me."

"Why?"

She sighs. "I think he feels I nag him about all the time he spends with the band."

I cock my head. "Does he know how much you miss him when you don't see him?"

"He must."

"But you haven't told him?"

"Not exactly."

I point to one of Brains's points and read it out to her. "Number eight: blah, blah, blah . . . 'if we've done something wrong, tell us. We're not mind readers.'" I look at her. "See! Tell him how you feel."

She stares down at her hands and twists the butterfly ring on her finger. "It's not as easy as that."

"Why not?"

"Look, I don't want to lose him, OK? And music means everything to him; it's his life. If I push him too far, maybe he'll choose music over me."

"You really think he'd do that?"

She shrugs. "Maybe."

"Clover, you're crazy. He's mad about you. Even I can see that. Just talk to him, please?"

She looks up and blows the air out of her mouth in a whoosh. "You're right. I need to find out one way or the other. Not knowing is killing me." She pauses. "Speaking of errant boys, any news from Mills yet?"

"Yep. Your plan worked. Eriq's super keen again. Only she's not sure she likes him now."

"Seriously? After all our cracking advice? What a waste."

"Yep. She got an e-mail from Bailey—this new guy in school—and now she's confused. I basically told her we've done all we can and she's on her ownio with this one."

Clover whistles. "When it comes to boys, Mills is one mixed-up cookie. This does not bode well for her future. But it will give us a heck of a lot of fab agony aunt material, Bean Machine."

"Clover!"

She just grins.

I sleep through most of the flight, as does Clover, not surprisingly. When we arrive, a taxi ferries us from Charles de Gaulle Airport to the center of Paris via the motorway. The taxi driver keeps his window fully open, his tanned arm resting on the sill. It's a bit windy in the back, but Clover and I don't mind. (Mum's dozing and Monique's in the front.)

Paris is much sunnier than Dublin, but not as warm as I'd expected. The air smells different, crisper, and it catches at the back of the throat. Dad claims every city has its own special scent — New York smells of hot metal: sparkly, exciting. Dublin smells musty, like damp washing. (He's not wrong there!)

For a while, there isn't much to see. Just some huge advertising billboards and lots of other taxis buzzing in and out of the fast-moving traffic, like summer hornets. Then a hill appears to our left, a big white building gleaming at its summit.

"Voilà!" Monique says, pointing at it. "The Sacré Cœur. We're nearly in Montmartre. Not far now."

Clover grabs my hand in excitement and we grin at each other like loons.

♥ Chapter 22

We arrive at Hôtel Unique: an impressive white-stone townhouse with smart black canvas shades over its large sash windows and miniature olive trees in pots at the front door. It's beautiful, tucked away down a shady lane right in the thick of Montmartre's winding cobblestone streets that are full of ultrastylish shops, dinky houses, and bijoux apartments. Perfect.

Gazing at the hotel, I clutch Clover's arm and beam at her. She smiles back.

"I think Saffy did us proud, girls," Monique says.

The friendly dark-haired concierge, who looks only a little bit older than Clover, greets us in the small lobby, then helps us lug our bags up the narrow staircase. (It's pretty old, so it doesn't have a lift.) On the way up, she tells us about the hotel.

"There are only five bedrooms in Hôtel Unique," she says with an accent I can't quite place, but it sounds familiar, "and each is decorated in the style of a different French artist — Monet, Degas, Renoir, Matisse, and Morisot —"

"Are you Irish?" Clover interrupts suddenly.

The concierge smiles. "Half. My mother's from Donegal; Dad's from Brittany. I know I have a funny accent. We Irish pop up everywhere, don't we?" She shows us to our rooms and then says, "Enjoy your stay. Let me know if you need anything."

Mum and Monique are sharing the Degas room. It has antique tutus hanging on the walls — very theatrical — it suits Monique perfectly. Clover and I are in the Matisse, which is complete with exotic slate-blue and orange walls and has its own mosaic hammam, or steam room.

We dump our bags and go back to Mum and Monique's room to have a nosy around. Remembering the concierge's description of the other rooms, I ask, "Mum, who's Morisot?"

"Berthe Morisot was one of France's most successful female impressionists," she says.

"Like me," Clover says. "Guess who this is." She hitches up her shorts so the waistband is practically under her armpits. "Hate it. Awful, awful, awful. My dog's better than you are, mate. You've got no talent whatsoever."

"Simon Cowell," I say with a grin. "The shorts gave it away."

Mum rolls her eyes. "Not that kind of impressionist, Clover. A painter."

We all roll around the place laughing.

After a rather boozy lunch in the hotel's tree-dappled courtyard, Mum yawns and stretches her arms over her head.

"I'm whacked," she says. "Think I'll potter upstairs for a little *siesta*."

Monique nods. "Good idea, Sylvie. Traveling is so exhausting. I'll join you."

"Party poopers," Clover says.

"Maybe you should have a rest too, Amy," Mum suggests.

"Absolutely out of the question." Clover grabs my hand and pulls me to my feet. "Things to do and people to see. I'll take good care of her, Sylvie. *À bientôt*."

Before Mum has a chance to protest, Clover drags me up the side steps that lead to the front of the hotel, down the stepping-stone path, and out the black iron gate.

We stand in the lane, look at each other, and then start laughing.

"Ready to put your plan into action, French Bean?" Clover wiggles her eyebrows.

I nod. *"Oui, mademoiselle."*

"Oh, *très bien*, Beanie. *Très bien.*"

She hooks my arm and runs me down the cobblestoned slope, fast. At the bottom we collapse in a giggling heap. Clover holds my head in the crook of her arm and runs her knuckles over my scalp. "Noggin, noggin, noggin," she says, rubbing hard.

"Ow, Clover!" I pull away and massage my skull. "Have you gone mad? That hurt."

She beams at me. "I'm just so psyched to be here, Beanie! And I already heart Paris so much." She crosses her arms tightly, then turns her back to me and moves her hands up and down her own shoulders and back, so it looks like someone is hugging her.

I laugh. "You're such a big kid. Seth does that too."

She jumps around and sits on her hands. "Ah, Sethy-baby. So what about tonight? If all goes well, do you think you'll be spending this evening with lover boy?"

"I hope so. But until I talk to him, I can't say for sure. Got your satnav?"

215 ♥

She pats her bag. "Yep. Just as well Brains believes in such ultraromantic presents. Let me see: a Memory Stick, a new hands-free kit, this satnav yoke . . ." She counts them off on her fingers and laughs. "I do wish he'd buck the trend and give me perfume or underwear sometimes."

"Seth writes me poetry," I say without thinking. *Siúcra*, he'll kill me.

"Cute. Any good?"

"Yes," I say loyally. "But Brains did fix your laptop that time it crashed. It must be pretty handy having a computer guru on tap."

"Guess so. Now, ready to implement the spyware?"

"Abso-doodle-utely. I can't wait to see Seth's face. How long have we got until Mum sends out a search party?"

"Ages. Did you see the beds? Comfy as Little Bear's. She'll be Goldilocks until dinnertime. Right, let's put Operation Seth into action."

She takes out her satnav, flicks it on, and stares down at the screen. Attached to the side like a Memory Stick is a box about the size of a matchbox. A red light is flickering and flashing intermittently, and it's making a beeping noise.

"I still can't believe people really invent things like this."

"I know, and isn't this a fab way of running a consumer test for the mag?" Her eyes sparkle. "Couldn't be more perfect."

"So how does it work again?" I ask.

"You plant the special pen in your boyfriend's — in this case, Seth's — bag and attach the tracking device to any satnav system. Genius."

I feel a bit uneasy. "I hope Seth doesn't mind us tracking him. It's kind of like spying, isn't it?"

"Duh! That's why it's called the Spy on Your Boyfriend Kit. Where's your sense of adventure? Besides, you can't back out now, Beanie. I promised Saffy a feature."

"A feature? On what?"

"Tracking your errant boyfriend, of course. This spy kit's expensive. Saffy only let me borrow it on the condition that I do a three-hundred-word review and work it into a piece. Saffy's very keen on this whole spy kit shebang — I think the company must be putting an ad into the mag or something."

"Seth's not errant," I protest.

She shrugs. "He will be in my piece."

"He'd better be completely unrecognizable, Clover. I'm warning you."

"Settle your tights, Beanie. I'm not stupid. And it's not like he reads the *Goss*, is it?"

She has a point.

"OK," she says, staring at the screen. "It's picking up his signal — he's on Boulevard du Palais."

"Is that near?"

Clover makes a face. "Not exactly. We'll grab a taxi."

Luckily, it doesn't take too long to hail one, and we're soon bouncing along in the backseat, our eyes glued to the screen, following the little red dot along the street map. The device is making a beeping noise at regular intervals, like a chirping chick. *Beep, beep, beep.*

"He's just crossed the river at Pont au Change," Clover says. "Now he's turned onto Rue de Rivoli. We're going the wrong way!" She gabbles a few words in French to the taxi driver, who grunts, nods once, indicates, and throws the cab into a U-ey, the tires screeching on the asphalt.

"*Merci, monsieur,*" she says, giving him a winning smile.

He grunts again. (Her school French is coming in pretty useful.)

"It's like being in a cop movie," she whispers. We're both trying not to giggle.

Minutes later, as we cross the Pont au Change,

the beeps start to get louder and closer together. And then suddenly there's just one almost continuous *BEEEEEEP*.

"Stop! *Arett-ey*-something!" Clover squeals.

The taxi driver spits out a word in French that sounds pretty rude and then does an emergency stop. We're flung forward and my chest thumps against the seat belt.

"You OK, Beanie?" Clover looks at me a little sheepishly.

I nod, but before I can answer, the taxi driver has spun around and is ranting and throwing his hands around in the air.

"What's he saying?" I ask Clover.

She concentrates. "'Are you crazy?'" she translates. "'Are you trying to kill us all?'"

She says something back to him in French and shows him the satnav and the red dot.

"*Ah, oui?*" he says, his face softening. "*Méchant garçon.*" His bushy eyebrows shoot up and he gives a fruity chuckle.

I don't know that much French, but I think *méchant* means "naughty," and I know *garçon* means "boy." Poor Seth. I won't have him disparaged by random French taxi drivers.

"Clover, what did you say to him?" I demand. "Seth hasn't done anything wrong. I just want to surprise him, that's all."

Clover says something else to the taxi driver and he just laughs. I give up and push open the cab door huffily, leaving Clover to pay the fare.

We've pulled up beside an open square in front of a modern building covered with giant striking LEGO-colored plastic tubes.

"How perfect!" I say, staring at the building. "He's definitely in there."

Clover stands beside me, her nose wrinkling. "What? Inside that load of old scaffolding? But wait . . . it does look familiar."

"That, Miss Art Philistine, is the Pompidou Centre. One of the best modern-art galleries in the world." I feel a rush of excitement, from the tips of my toes to my hair follicles; it's so intense it gives me goose bumps. I couldn't have picked a better place to rendezvous if I'd tried. Seth and I have both shared the same dream all our lives: to visit the MoMA in New York and the Pompidou in Paris.

"You OK to take it from here, Bean Machine?" Clover asks gently.

I nod. "Think so."

"I've turned down the sound, so as soon as the red light goes solid, he'll be right in front of you," she says, handing over the spy kit. "I'll meet you back here in an hour. *Bon courage*, Beanie," she adds, kissing her fingers and blowing them at me.

♥ Chapter 23

I have to keep saying, "Holy Moly, I'm in the Pompidou Centre," over and over and over under my breath as I walk in the doors. I can't help it. Inside, I head straight for the loos at the back of the enormous lobby. All the anticipation is getting to me. After weeing — twice — I wash my hands and stare in the mirror over the sink.

A new zit flashes proudly from my chin. Typical! I resist the urge to poke or squeeze it. I'm not alone, and although I've seen people do far weirder things in public loos — like pluck hairy moles (honestly!) — I'm not that much of an odd-let. Instead, I whip out my Rimmel cover stick and try to repair the damage.

When I'm done, I take a deep breath, wipe my damp hands on my jeans (those hand-dryer things never work properly), brush my hair back, pop on Clover's New York Yankees cap, and slide my sunglasses over my eyes — my disguise is complete! I walk back out into the lobby, and while I queue for my ticket, I can feel my heartbeat quicken and my palms breaking out in a sticky sweat. By the time I walk through the turnstiles, my stomach is roller-coaster lurching and I'm beginning to wish I hadn't eaten that second croque-monsieur at lunch. (But for such a simple sambo — basically just fancy cheese on toast — it was delicious.)

Just then, the satnav gives a little beep, and I move to the side of the corridor, away from the yabbering tourists, to check it. The red light is almost constant now, but where is he? I look up and down the corridor but there's no sign of him. I hadn't realized the gallery would be quite so big. I look down at the map that the lady in the ticket booth handed me.

Knowing Miss Lupin, she's probably told her French class they can go anywhere they like, as long as they meet her back in the lobby at a certain time. She's decent that way. My money's on Mills and some of the other girls spending most of the time in the café, people (i.e., *boy*) watching.

But it's Seth I'm interested in right now. I can catch up with Mills later. Where would *he* go? My eye lingers over a certain painter's name and — bingo! — I know exactly where I'll find him: LEVEL 5: FROM 1905 TO 1960.

I make my way up the escalator, gripping the moving handle for dear life. I'm not a great fan of heights, and the escalators are housed on the outside of the building, in giant glass tubes that look down on the bustling piazza. I look at the square for a second, seeing if I can pick out Clover, but immediately start to feel dizzy, so sweep my eyes away again.

At level 5, I jump off the escalator and check the satnav. The red light is almost solid, just flickering a tiny bit, like dodgy Christmas lights, and as I walk around the corner, it goes solid red. I look up. I was right. Room 40: abstract expressionism; Jackson Pollock and . . . Mark Rothko — our favorite artist.

I peer in the doorway — and there he is: Seth. Even with his back to me, I'd recognize him anywhere. He's staring at the extraordinary huge black-and-red canvas like his life depended on it, not moving an inch. I watch him for a moment, emotions washing through me. I'm so happy to see him, but nervous too. Maybe Mills was right: maybe surprising him wasn't such a brilliant idea. But it's too late now.

I take off my sunglasses and study the canvas, drinking in the dense, sooty-black rectangle floating over a smaller red rectangle, feeling the intense emotion behind the painting so strongly I can almost taste Rothko's anger, loneliness, and despair. There's another Rothko — three brown boxes against a black background — on the left-hand wall, but it's the red painting that really sucks you in. I can see why Seth is so transfixed.

I'm hesitating, wondering whether to just run away, when, as if sensing my gaze, Seth slowly turns around. Our eyes meet and for a second his face is blank, then slowly realization seems to dawn on him. "It's really you," he says eventually, staring at me in shock.

I nod, smiling nervously. "Surprise!" The moment it's out, I regret opening my mouth. It sounds stupid, like something a child would say at a birthday party.

He shakes his head. "I don't understand."

"I flew over this morning. With Mum and Clover and Mum's friend Monique. We're shopping for bridesmaids' dresses."

"How did you find me?" He doesn't seem all that pleased to see me, and I'm starting to feel a little anxious.

"Clover's satnav. We hooked it up to a tracking device — a special pen that Mills planted in your backpack." I say it quickly without thinking, but as soon as the words tumble out, I realize how kooky it must sound. Maybe I should have kept my mouth shut, or lied — told him I'd been talking to Mills or something.

"Tracking device?" He looks at me incredulously. "You've been *following* me?"

I shrug. "I know it sounds a bit weird."

"A bit? Try completely freakoid. Stalking people isn't normal, Amy. How long have you been watching me?"

"Not long. I just wanted to know where to find you."

"You could have just rung and asked me. And what about Polly? You said you'd be there if she needed anything. You promised."

My face falls.

"Didn't think of that, did you?" he says bitterly.

"No," I say in a tiny voice, my stomach dropping into my shoes. "Dave's at home this weekend, though," I add a bit desperately. "I could ring him, ask him to keep —"

"You have an answer for everything, don't you, Amy?" He has a hurt, angry look on his face that makes my heart shrivel up like a salted slug. "Just once I wish you'd —"

"Ah, Seth. There you are," says a voice behind me.

Yikes, it's Miss Lupin — that's all I need.

Luckily, I have my back to her, so, throwing my sunglasses back on, I take a few steps away from Seth. (Dave told Mrs. Peacock, the school secretary, that I was attending an important family reunion in England today, and I don't want to get him into trouble.)

"I was looking for you, Seth," Miss Lupin says. "Do hurry along. The film about Calder's *Circus* is about to start. I asked everyone to meet outside Cinema One ten minutes ago. You're the last of my little lost sheep, apart from Annabelle Hamilton. But I've given up on her. Probably a blessing." She walks back into the corridor.

"Seth," I say when she's gone. "Can't we—"

He just shrugs. "You heard the teach. Better go. And it's not like you can't find me again with your little boyfriend-tracker."

"But—" I'm flabbergasted. This isn't how our romantic meeting in Paris is supposed to end. He's supposed to sweep me into his arms, kiss me, and tell me how clever I am to have found him . . . not this damp squib of a reunion.

He ignores me and heads for the door.

Miss Lupin is waiting for him outside. "Who was that?" I hear her ask as they walk away together.

"Just a girl who likes Rothko," he says. "No one special."

♥ Chapter 24

When we get back from the Pompidou Centre, I flop down on my hotel bed and lie there, staring up at the slate-blue ceiling. Clover sits on the side of the bed and looks down at me. "Here's the thing, Beanie," she says. "You can either lie here all evening, wallowing in your misery like a hippo in mud, or you can forget about Seth and embrace the holiday regardless. We're in Paris, Beanie. *Paris!* So which is it to be: hippo or Paris?"

I groan. I know Clover has a point. I mean, we're in one of the most beautiful cities in the world and all I can think about is the mess with Seth. It's all of my own creation too, which just makes it a whole heap more difficult to bear. I've rung and texted him loads of times, but I've only received one miserly text back: C U BACK IN DUBLIN, AMY.

"Hippo or Paris?" I say. "I choose Paris."

Clover smiles. "That's the spirit, Beanie. Now, why don't you ring Mills — she might be able to cheer you up a bit. At the very least, you can have a giggle at her latest boy drama. You have her host family's number, don't you?"

I nod.

"Well, then, what are you waiting for?"

"What happens if Madame Barnard answers? What will I say?"

"I'm sure she speaks English, Beanie."

I pick at my nail nervously.

"Oh, I'll do it, then." Clover takes my mobile off me and rings the Barnards' number. She gabbles something in French, then hands the phone back to me with a smile.

"Think that may have been the bold Eriq-y-deek-deek. He's getting Mills for you."

"Thanks, Clover."

"No worries, mate," she says in her best Aussie accent. "I'm heading outside to soak up some rays in the outback. Catch you later, Sheila."

It takes a few seconds for Mills to come to the phone, but then she asks with concern, "Amy, is everything all right? What happened with Seth? He wouldn't tell me a thing, but he didn't seem all that smiley."

I'm so glad to hear her voice I instantly dissolve into tears. "It was a disaster! He thinks I'm a freak for stalking him, and he's really annoyed I abandoned Polly." I give a big hiccup of a sob.

"Ah, Ames, don't cry. We'll sort it out. Hang on a second." In the background, Mills says something in French. (She must be talking to one of the Barnards.) A second later, she's back. "I'm coming over there right now to give you a great big hug. Eriq knows where the hotel is. Stay right where you are."

"Oooo-kaaayyy," I wail.

I decide to wait for her in the lobby, and once I've stopped crying, I put on sunglasses to cover my blotchy eyes and head downstairs. I'm sitting on a sofa in the corner when I hear someone say, "Amy?"

I look up and there she is, Mills, with a boy loitering behind her who must be Eriq. She's right: on the dark-haired cute scale, he's right up there with Bailey and the Deppster.

Mills smiles down at me: a soft, gentle "I'm so sorry" smile, and I dissolve into tears again. Luckily,

I'm still wearing my dark glasses, and apart from Eriq, there's no one else in the lobby to see me.

"*Tu peux attendre dehors*, Eriq?" Mills says, without turning around.

"*Bien sûr*," he says, and disappears.

"Found yourself a new lapdog?" I ask, putting my sunglasses on the top of my head and brushing away my tears with the back of my hand.

She wrinkles up her nose. "I asked him to wait outside. I've gone right off him, to be honest — too clingy. But he did give me a lift over here on his crossbar, so I'd better be nice to him, I suppose."

"Thanks for coming."

"That's what friends are for." She sits down beside me on the sofa, and the leather makes a tiny farting noise. "Wasn't me." Her face colors a little.

I laugh through my tears. "'Course it wasn't. Mills Starr doesn't fart or sweat — she's far too perfect."

Mills shoves me with her shoulder. "Good to see you smiling again. How are you holding up?"

I shrug. "Been better. I'm such an idiot. I should have listened to you, Mills. It's all such a mess."

"Tell me everything. Start from when Seth first spotted you in the gallery."

I unfold the whole sorry tale, right up to the bit

where Seth walked off with Miss Lupin, saying I was no one special.

"Ouch!" Mills winces. "Poor you. Has he been in contact since?"

I show her his text.

She pats my hand. "Never mind, eh? At least he's not completely ignoring you."

I sigh. "I wish I'd never come here. Now every time I think of Paris, I'll feel sad. What a waste! Maybe I should just spend the rest of the holiday in my room."

"Don't say that, Amy. You have the whole weekend ahead of you. And what about Clover and your mum and Mad Monique? You don't want to ruin it for everyone, do you?"

"Guess not." I stare down at the marble floor, my glasses sliding down my hair. I take them off and hold them in my hands, turning them over and over.

"Try not to think about Seth, all right? You're going shopping tomorrow. That'll be fun. We're off to Versailles for the day, but I'll ring your mobile as soon as we get back. I'm sure the Barnards will let me use their phone. Mine doesn't work over here, as you know."

Mills is making such an effort, I force myself to be cheerful. "Thanks. Now, enough about me; heard anything else from Bailey?"

Her eyes light up. "Another PM. Says he's missing me. Swoon. Be still, my beating heart."

"Glad someone's romantic life is working out," I say glumly.

♥ Chapter 25

The following morning I open my eyes slowly, and once they're focused, I spot Clover curled up in the window seat in her pajamas, the window thrown open and the sun shining in. The air smells fresh and slightly sweet and citrusy, like an orange grove, and birds are chirping from the trees.

She looks over. "Beautiful morning, Beanie."

I push myself up in the bed and sit facing her. Then yesterday's disaster comes flooding back to me and I feel sick to my stomach.

"You all right?" she asks. "You look kinda groggy."

"Didn't sleep very well, tossing and turning all night."

"Nightmares?"

I nod.

"About what?" she asks.

"Can't really remember: something about running after someone. Oh, and drowning in a lake full of blood."

Clover lifts her eyebrows. "Nice."

I roll my stiff shoulders and groan a little. "I'm not sure I'm up to shopping today. Do you think Mum will mind if I stay here?"

She goes quiet and gazes out of the window for a moment before looking at me again and saying, "Beanie, I thought you'd chosen Paris over feeling miserable about Seth. What if this is your only visit to Paris, ever? I guarantee you'll spend the rest of your life regretting you didn't climb out of that bed and make the most it."

I frown. "That's just silly. 'Course I'll be here again."

"Maybe, maybe not. There are a lot of cities to cover in a lifetime, Bean Machine. Don't play Russian roulette with Paris." She puts down her mag and stands over me. "And don't make me drag you into the shower. Move!"

After breakfast (I manage half a croissant and some hot chocolate), Clover and I leave Mum and Monique sipping their third cups of coffee and discussing waxing versus shaving (fascinating stuff—not) and hit the shops. We promise to catch up with them later for bridesmaid-dress shopping.

After mooching in and out of some so-so boutiques, we find this cool place that sells end-of-the-line designer clothes. Clover finds a stunning Jean Paul Gaultier waistcoat for twenty euro and a pair of red skinny jeans with the label ripped out for next to nothing. We try on some eye-wateringly expensive leather jackets in another shop, parading up and down in front of the mirror and pretending to be rock chicks.

We just have time for a quick café lunch before we have to dash to meet Mum and Monique at the Place des Abbesses Métro sign. "There you are, girls." Monique beams at us.

Mum looks a little agitated. "You're ten minutes late."

"Loosen up, Sylvie," Clover says. "We're on holidays, remember?"

Before Mum has a chance to say anything else, Monique takes my hand and leads me down a quiet cobbled backstreet. "Keep up, you two!" she shouts at Clover and Mum.

"I thought we were supposed to be looking for bridesmaids' dresses?" Clover grumbles a few minutes later, after stubbing her big toe on a protruding cobblestone. "I don't see any shops."

Monique laughs as Clover grabs my arm and adjusts the strap of her shoe. "I did warn you not to wear heels."

Clover scowls. "Wedgies aren't heels. And I wanted to look my best for our visits to Chanel and Sonia Rykiel."

Mum frowns. "Clover, I don't have that kind of money. You know that."

"I wasn't suggesting *buying* our dresses there, Sylvie," Clover says. "I'm not *that* delusional. I just thought we could have a look, get wedding ideas, inspiration."

"For my simple not-too-much-fuss wedding?" Mum says, her eyebrows arching.

Monique claps her hands together. "Girls, do stop squabbling. We are here: L'Atelier Clair de Lune. In English: the Moonlight Workshop. Owned and run by one of my dearest friends, Odette Lune. Ta-da!" She throws her arms out theatrically. "What do you think?"

We all stare at the shop front. It is painted midnight blue, and sparkling white fairy lights frame both its plate-glass windows. "L'Atelier Clair de Lune" is written in curling white letters across the glass, and silvery-gray velvet curtains hide what's inside. It looks magical.

Monique pushes the door open, and there's a metallic click as the old-fashioned bell attached to the top of the door frame gives a *ting-a-ling-a-ling.*

It's just as enchanting inside—a work desk runs the whole way along the right-hand wall, and two large sewing machines sit proudly on the wood, like gunmetal swans. Above the machines is a shelf crammed with spools of rainbow thread and glass jars packed with buttons. On a second shelf are stacks of clear plastic boxes full of multicolored ribbon, velvet bows, silk butterflies, tiny metal clasps, and snow-white and owl-brown feathers. It's like a fashion candy store.

On the sound system, a strong, gravelly woman's voice is singing about regretting *rien* — which I think means "nothing."

"Amazing," Clover says, running her finger over a miniature gold top hat perched on top of a dressmaker's dummy.

The dress on the dummy is out of this world — a buttercup-yellow bustier encrusted with a delicate lacy pattern in gold embroidery sits above a skirt of pale-yellow chiffon layers that are shimmying in the slight draft.

The left-hand wall is alive with even more

incredible dresses, mostly delicate pastel colors, with the odd dash of hot pink or turquoise, all dancing on a steel rail.

"Wow, wow, wow!" Mum parades up and down the frocks, lost for words. She looks like Alex at the model-train museum, her eyes bugging in their sockets. Stopping in front of a delicate shell-pink dress, she unhooks its hanger from the rail and holds it up against me.

"You suggested pink for Amy, didn't you?" she asks Monique.

Monique nods. "Pink for Amy and green for me and Clover. But you have the final say, of course, Sylvie."

Mum looks me up and down. "I know you don't normally wear pink, but the color suits you perfectly. Look." She spins me around to look in the old-fashioned floor mirror by the work desk. Her eyes fill with tears.

I take the dress out of her hand, and holding it up against me, I stare in the mirror. For a second I don't recognize myself. It's not a shade I would have chosen, but I have to admit, it does make my skin glow. The boned bodice is a pale-pink raw silk, while the chiffon skirt, ballerina length but not too full, is a slightly darker pink.

As I'm looking at myself, a curtain twitches at the back of the shop and a blond girl steps out. She's even smaller than Clover, which is saying something, and is dressed head to toe in black, from her lacy shirt to her patent brogues. Her neat chignon and the slash of ruby red on her lips make her look like a 1930s movie star. She smiles at me. *"Vous voulez l'essayer?"*

And then she notices Monique. "Monny!" She throws her arms around her friend. *"Ça me fait bien plaisir de te voir!"*

"Detty!" They hug and hug and hug, laughing and dancing on the spot and prattling away in French.

I grin at Clover. "Think that'll be us when we're ancient?"

She smiles back. "I hope so." Then, lowering her voice, she asks, "Do you really like the dress?" (She knows it's not my usual style.)

"It's pretty," I whisper back. "And it's Mum's day."

Odette finally draws away from Monique, and turning to Mum, she smiles. "And you must be Sylvie. I 'ear much about you from Monny. And you're getting *married*. How wonderful!" Her eyes sparkle and she looks genuinely thrilled for Mum. "Monny say you look for bridesmaids' dresses, yes?"

"That's right," Mum says. "For my daughter Amy."

She puts her hand on my shoulder. "And Monny and Clover. Clover's my sister."

Odette looks surprised. "Yes? You look very different."

Clover grins. "Thanks."

Mum gives her a thump on the arm.

"Hey!" Clover squeals, rubbing her skin.

"So three dresses in total," Mum adds, ignoring her. "And I just love this one." She points at the pink dress I'm still holding. "Can Amy try it on?"

"Of course." Odette leads me into the changing room and leaves me to get undressed. Once I've slipped the dress on, the silk soft and deliciously cool against my skin, I stare in the mirror. The bodice is way too big, my boobs don't go near filling it, but the waist fits perfectly. The dress dips low at the back to just below my shoulder blades. It's not only my nose and chin that have broken out in spots, there's a new crop tattooing my right shoulder blade, and the way things are going, my skin will be even worse by Mum's wedding on New Year's Eve. I can wear makeup on my face, but what about my back?

"Ready, Amy?" Mum calls through the changing-room curtain.

I take a deep breath, part the curtain, and walk out, my shoulders hunched a little in embarrassment.

Mum doesn't seem to notice. Her hands flutter to her chest as she practically swoons. "Amy, you look beautiful — like Cinderella."

I grin and pull at the bodice. "I could certainly keep a coach team of mice and lizards down the front."

Odette laughs. "That is easily fixed. When do you leave, tomorrow?"

Monique says, "Sadly, yes. Tomorrow evening."

"Boo!" I add.

Odette smiles at me. "You like my city?"

I nod eagerly. "It's amazing."

"That makes me very 'appy. Now, a few tucks and the dress will be perfect. And I will 'ave it ready tomorrow afternoon, yes?" Odette slips a small velvet pincushion on a thick black elastic band onto the back of her hand and ushers me into the changing room. "Come, come." Once inside she begins gathering and pinning the bodice. (I'm afraid to move in case I get prickled in the chest by one of the pearl-topped pins.)

When she moves around to the back, I wince and my shoulders stiffen. Odette will be appalled by the state of my skin. Her dress deserves better. And I'll be even more exposed walking up the aisle in front of Mum. Absolutely everyone will see my spots then.

It'll ruin the day for me, I just know it. Oh, why did I agree to be a bridesmaid in the first place? I blink frantically, trying not to cry.

Odette smooths the back of the bodice with her hands, puts in two more small tucks, and then stands in front of me again and smiles. "Looks good. Nearly done." Then she notices my wobbling lips. "My dear, what's wrong? You 'ate my dress?"

I shake my head. "No, it's gorgeous. It's just . . . I feel uncomfortable showing so much bare flesh. . . . My skin's so bad. . . . I'm sorry." I start to cry.

Odette digs in her pocket and hands me a pale-blue cotton handkerchief, with a tiny moon embroidered in one corner. She folds it into my hand. "I made it myself. Is yours now. Clean, I promise." She smiles.

I smile back and use it to mop up my tears. "Thank you. I'm so sorry. You must think I'm being ridiculous."

"Not at all. I tell you a story. When I was about your age I 'ad terrible acne, all down 'ere. And 'ere." She runs her fingers down her neck and then points at the top of her chest. "And all over my back. I 'ated it — so embarrassing. I made my mother give me a note to get off games and gym so I wouldn't 'ave to change in front of the other girls. That makes me sad now — it was so extreme. But it seemed like the only option at the time.

"I was desperate to 'ide my skin. I couldn't find any clothes I liked, so I started to make my own. I got quite good at it, and now you see I 'ave my own shop. So to every dark cloud there is a silver lining. You 'ave a few spots, my dear, but they are 'ardly noticeable. To you they seem unsightly, 'ideous, yes?"

I nod. "Yes. Revolting."

"Really they are very small. And your skin will clear up in time. But for now, be clever with what you wear. And for this dress, I 'ave a solution." She disappears out of the changing room for a second and comes back with a cute green silk cropped jacket dusted with darker green sequins, which she pops over my shoulders. She then ties a matching sash around my waist.

"For good luck," she adds, fastening a tiny gold-and-green frog brooch onto the right-hand side of the bodice. "Now take another look."

I stare in the mirror again. The bodice fits like a glove, and now that I'm not fretting about people staring at my back, I feel like a million dollars.

"We show the others?" Odette says. "Yes?"

"Yes! Thank you, Odette." I give her a hug.

"My pleasure. You make my dress come to life,

Amy. Thank *you*." She shakes her head. "I am so glad I am not a teenager anymore. Is difficult, yes? But fun."

I laugh. "You said it."

When I walk out of the changing room, even Clover is impressed. She whistles. "Not bad, Beanie. And the jacket and sash really funk up the whole look. I love Kermit." She fingers the tiny frog, then turns to the silver rails and pulls out a mint-green version of the same dress. "What do you think of this one for me?" She holds it up against her chest.

"I like it," I say. "It suits you."

"Try it with this." Odette hands her a hot-pink jacket and sash. Clover doesn't look all that convinced but toddles off to try it on.

"Stay in your dress, Amy," Mum says, "and we'll see how they work together."

"How do I look?" Clover asks, sashaying out of the changing room a few minutes later. She's flicking the skirt around with her hand, and unlike me, she fills the bodice beautifully.

"Stunning," Odette says.

Again, Mum is so overcome she can barely speak. She waves her hand in front of her face, smiles, and nods, her eyes damp.

"Amy?" Clover turns to me. "Be honest."

"Like a princess."

Clover looks at Monique.

"*Très chic,*" Monique says. "Both of you. Now, stand together, girls, so I can take some photos. Vogue, darlings. Like real models."

Clover straightens her back, tosses her hair around, and pouts for the camera. I copy her, and Monique laughs.

Meanwhile, Mum is wiping away the last of her tears and hugging Odette. "I thought finding a dress for Clover would be a nightmare. She's so hard to please. I had visions of her trooping up the aisle in a Lycra mini or a pair of shorts. Thank you, thank you, thank you. I'm so grateful."

"Sylvie!" Clover complains. "That's charming. I don't wear Lycra minis." (Which is a total lie.)

Mum and I swap a knowing look.

"And for Monny." Odette whips a dress off the end of a rail and peels back a layer of plastic. There is a red ribbon on the top of the hanger, Monique's name dangling off it on a brown luggage label. (Mum has some ideas about her own dress — she doesn't want it to be too fussy — but she's refusing to commit to anything yet.)

Odette holds the dress up in front of Monique, and we all gasp. The unusual moss-green silk, sprinkled with dark-pink sequins, suits her pale skin tone perfectly. It has a sleeker silhouette than our dresses, but the three colors work beautifully together. Odette is a genius.

"I 'ope you like it, Monny," she adds.

"Like it?" Monique gives Odette another hug. "I love it!"

Monique tries it on immediately, and when she stalks out of the changing room like a supermodel, head held high, we all clap and cheer.

"It's stunning, Monny," Odette says. "If I do say so myself. You do it proud, my dear friend."

Monique kisses her on both cheeks.

"What do you think, Sylvie?" Monique asks.

Once again, Mum's lost for words — but judging by the blissed-out look on her face, I think it's safe to say she approves. It's only after Monique has changed and come back out of the changing room that Mum finds her tongue.

"So we can collect the dresses tomorrow afternoon?" she asks Odette. "And pay for them, of course." A slight shadow falls over her face — even with the upcoming ghostwriting job, I know she's worried about how she's going to afford the wedding.

Odette pats Mum's hand. "Do not worry. Monique 'as something to tell you."

Monique looks at Mum. "They're a present," she says, "from me to you. For being the best friend a girl could wish for. Besides, Odette gave me a whopping discount!"

Mum's eyes well up again and she hugs Monique. "I do love you, Monny. And thank you so much too, Odette," she calls over Monique's shoulder.

Clover grins. "Once you've all finished your mutual admiration love-in, can we please hit Sonia Rykiel and Chanel? Just to look. We only have one more day in Paris and I've hardly seen any shops at all."

"Oooh, can I come?" Odette squeals. "*J'adore* Chanel. So stylish. I love trying on the little suits and pretending to be rich enough to buy them."

"You will be one day," Clover says. "Your dresses are amazing."

"Thank you, *ma chérie*." Odette strokes Clover's cheek.

"What about the shop?" Monique asks.

Odette smiles. "The joy of working for yourself. I 'ave a special sign." And Odette hands her a rectangular card.

Monique translates the swirling red script for the rest of us. " 'Fashion emergency,' " she reads. " 'Back later.' "

Once she has fastened it to the door, Odette claps her hands together. "There. Now, take me shopping." She hooks Clover's arm on one side and Monique's on the other.

Mum and I join the line and we all march down the street, singing "Here Come the Girls," and laughing so much we almost fall over.

And for a moment I forget Seth Stone even exists.

♥ Chapter 26

A combination of shopping and several raspberry-colored cocktails wipes out Mum and Monique, and they head straight to bed after dinner.

"Fancy a walk, Bean Machine? It's a beautiful evening," Clover says once the olds have excused themselves.

I smile. "That sounds perfect."

We head upstairs to our room and I sit on the bed, waiting for her to change her shoes and use the loo. I take my mobile out of my pocket and stare at the screen. Nothing. I haven't had a text from Seth all day. I start to feel a little mopey again but shake myself out of it — if that's how he wants to play it, fine.

But my fingers start to twitch a little. It wouldn't hurt to send him one little text, would it? Before I change my mind, I run my fingers over the keypad: WISH THINGS COULD BE DIFFERENT. THINKING OF U. AMY.

Seconds later, there's a beep.

"That my phone?" Clover calls from the bathroom.

"No, mine." My heart's hammering in my chest. It has to be from Seth. And I'm too nervous to read it.

"Is it Mills?"

"Nah, her mobile doesn't work over here."

Clover walks out of the loo, Tweezerman still clutched in her hand. "Seth?" she asks.

I shrug. "I don't know. Maybe."

"Read it, you eejit."

I say a quick prayer and look down. MAY HAVE OVERREACTED. 'POLOGIES. WHAT R U UP 2? CAN I C U L8R? Tears of relief spring to my eyes.

"That bad?" Clover asks.

Wordlessly, I hand her my phone and she reads the text. "Hey, Beanie, that's coola boola. A romantic makeup is defo in the cards. Where are you going to meet him? Has to be somewhere spectacular." She gasps and then grins. "I've got it, Beanie! The perfect location. Pont des Arts."

"*Pont?* Doesn't that mean 'bridge'?"

Clover just smiles mysteriously. "You'll get it, Beanie. Trust me."

I'm so nervous in the taxi I can barely breathe, let alone talk, so I just listen to Clover chatter on. "Isn't Odette amazing? The things she can do with silk chiffon. We're going to look like movie stars in our dresses. I know I was a bit hesitant at first, but they're fab. So, what about a matching hot-pink-and-green theme for the flowers and maybe for the cupcake icing? Any thoughts on that, Beanie? Are you even listening to me?"

" 'Course. Hot-pink-and-green flowers. And cupcake icing. Lovely jubbly."

She seems happy and starts talking again, so I tune out and stare out of the window until the taxi pulls up along the riverbank. "Pont des Arts," the driver says.

We climb out, and while Clover pays the fare, I walk toward the low stone wall overlooking the Seine. Putting my hands on the cool stone, I stare at the brightly lit iron pedestrian bridge cutting across the river. And then I recognize it and grin.

"Clover!" I say when she joins me. "It's where Carrie and Big meet in the last episode of *Sex and the City*."

"Correct. *Deux points*. And I think I see lover boy." She points at the bridge.

I follow her finger. It's early evening and the sky

has begun to darken. A row of old-fashioned *The Lion, the Witch and the Wardrobe* streetlights run on either side of the bridge's railings, and I pick out a lone figure about halfway across, sitting on a bench and staring out at the water. She's right: it's Seth. He's wearing a navy-and-white-checked shirt I haven't seen before. My stomach lurches. I hope I don't mess this up too.

"I'll just take a little walk along the river," Clover says. "Leave you lovebirds to it."

"On your own? What if you get mugged?"

She laughs. "It's crawling with tourists, Beanie. Besides, apart from a few euro, I have nothing worth taking. See you back here in, what, half an hour?"

I nod. "Wish me luck."

"*Bon courage.*" She kisses her fingers, blows them at me, and walks away.

I stand still for a few minutes, watching Seth and "plucking up gumption," as Gran would have said. I'm so nervous, my hands are shaking. Get a grip, Amy, I tell myself. It's only Seth.

Suddenly, he turns his head and looks at me. I can't quite make out his expression, but I think he's smiling. OK, Amy, that's a good sign. But my stomach lurches again. *Please make this work out,* I pray. *Please, please, please.*

I wave and he waves back and then stands up. I

start walking toward him over the wooden planks of the bridge, slowly at first, but picking up speed as soon as I make out the big smile plastered across his face. He starts running toward me, his runners making a slapping noise on the wood, and within seconds I'm in his arms, drinking in his familiar lemony smell, my face pressed against his shoulder.

"I'm so sorry," I say, my voice muffled a little by his shirt. "I should have told you I was coming to Paris."

He pulls away. "I'm the one who should be sorry. I was an idiot to push you away like that in the Pompidou Centre. We could have snuck off and had an amazing time. What a waste." He shakes his head.

"Can we start again?" I suggest.

He nods and takes my hand in his. "OMG, Amy, I can't believe, like, we're in Paris, like, together. It's so totally awesome."

I laugh. "Great D4 impression."

He bows. "I aim to please. But seriously, I'm so psyched you're here. And what a cool place to meet. Some bridge." He whistles.

"Clover's idea," I admit. Not being a *Sex and the City* fan, Seth hasn't copped the exact significance of the location; I toy with telling him, then decide against it. I want him to remember it as the Amy-and-Seth bridge. So I just smile instead.

"Clover?" He looks around. "Don't tell me she's spying on us."

"No, she and her tracking kit are far, far away."

"Good." He chuckles like an old movie villain. "I have dastardly plans that no human eye must see." He wiggles his eyebrows at me and then winks. "But first, a kiss from my leading lady, please." He puts his arms around me again and pulls me close. Our mouths lock—the kiss is passionate, almost fierce. It makes my head spin and my blood pump through my veins, fast. And just when I think I can't take any more, the pace slows, with lots of licks and nips and tiny kisses, and I feel soft and melty all over. It's the best kiss ever, and as we draw apart, I grin at Seth, then bury my head in his shirt, slightly embarrassed by the whole thing. I heard little groaning noises during the kiss; and I think they were from me. Oops. Cringe-a-rama!

He strokes the top of my head. "God, I've missed you, Amy," he says softly.

When I finally lift my head, he takes my hand and leads me toward one of the benches. We sit down and he throws his arm around my shoulders and draws me closer until our thighs and hips are pressed together. I can feel the heat of his body through my jeans.

We sit there for a while, saying nothing. A few people pass us—a tall slim woman in a black jumpsuit and biker boots walking a white poodle, a fit-looking man rollerblading, a bald man pushing a sleeping baby in a buggy. It's peaceful until a riverboat glides toward us, French pop music blaring out over the speakers. The guide says something and the passengers stand up to take photos. Seth and I both wave and then laugh as some of them wave back.

"So how was the palace?" I ask when the boat has passed. "You were at Versailles today, right?"

He shrugs. "Big. Lots of gold. All a bit *Footballers' Wives*, to be honest. But I liked the fountains. And the art. What did you get up to?"

I tell him about my day, leaving out the bit about Clover having to motivate me to get out of bed.

He grins. "Bridesmaids' dresses, eh? Fluffy pink meringues?"

"Hey!" I give him a playful slap. "How dare you? They're very tasteful."

Seth's still smiling.

"I don't know why you're grinning," I say. "You'll have to wear a suit and tie to the wedding."

"I'm invited?" He looks surprised.

"If you behave yourself, then yes . . . and as long as we're still together, of course."

He sits up a little, a frown clouding his face. "Are you trying to tell me something, Amy?"

"What? No, of course not. Things happen."
I shrug. "You know. You might get bored of me or something. Find someone else. Break my achy breaky heart." I give a short laugh, but Seth remains quiet. He seems unsettled, nervous.

Eventually he says, "There's something important I need to tell you. . . ."

My mind goes into overdrive. "Has something happened to Polly?" I texted Dave to ask whether Polly could call him if she needed anything, and it turned out that he'd already been checking up on her.

"No, nothing like that. Polly's grand. I spoke to her earlier and she said that Dave's been ringing her every day, visited the house and everything. He's really decent, isn't he?"

I nod. Seth's right: Dave's OK.

"Then what is it, Seth?" I ask. "What's wrong?"

He stares at me, eyes boring into mine. "Why did you say that stuff about me breaking your heart? Why would I break your heart? Just the thought of having to live without you kills me. I'm not going to hurt *you*. . . . But I've seen the way you look at Bailey. I know it's just a matter of time. He'd look far better on your arm at the wedding than I would, anyway. I don't even own a suit."

I'm too shocked to laugh. "Bailey? Seriously?

OK, yes, I look at him — it's hard not to with those cheekbones — but it's you I want to be with, Seth. It's always been you. Now, at the wedding, next year, the year after that. Always."

"You say that now, but you'll change your mind."

"I won't. I swear it, Seth. Why are you being like this? What's wrong?"

His eyes are fiery. "Don't you get it, Amy? I love you."

And the whole world just stops. I feel like I've been pushed underwater: everything is muffled and all I can think about are those three words — "I LOVE YOU."

How can such small words change so much, so quickly? My heart is threatening to hammer out of my chest, and my mouth is dry. Seth is still staring at me, a strange expression on his face. I try to say something but my lips won't move.

Suddenly he stands up and starts walking quickly across the bridge.

"Seth! Wait!" I cry, dashing after him.

He ignores me and dashes across the road without looking. He's almost mowed down by a cyclist.

"Seth!" I cry again. Then, while he's still just about in earshot, I shout, "I love you too! Can you hear me? I said I love you. Come back. Please come back."

He stops dead and stands with his back toward me. Eventually, he turns around and walks toward me. "You don't have to say it just 'cos I did," he says, a little out of breath. "If you don't feel the same . . ."

"But I do. I love you, Seth Stone. Which must make me super crazy."

He studies my face for a second, then breaks into a smile. "Say it again."

I start to sing Seth this old 1950s song the Red Hot Chili Peppers covered called "A Teenager in Love," a song I know makes him smile. "'Each time we have a quarrel, / It almost breaks my heart. / 'Cos I'm so afraid, / That we will have to part. / Each night I ask the stars up above, / Why must I be a teenager in love?'"

I can't really sing, but from the beam on his face, I think he gets the message. He sweeps me into his arms and flings me backward, my spine arching. Then he kisses me again.

"And I love you, Amy Green," he whispers, kissing my cheeks, my eyelids, the tip of my nose. "And will love you. Forever." And finally he kisses my lips. I close my eyes.

♥ Chapter 27

The following morning we manage to kidnap Mills. Yeah! Eriq told his parents he was taking her sightseeing, and Seth spun a similar story to his host family. They both have to be back before lunch to pack and catch the coach to the airport, but until then we have a few hours, just the three of us. We're sitting outside a café in the Jardin des Tuileries, shooting the breeze in the dappled shade of the trees, after a visit to the Louvre. Seth insisted I see the *Mona Lisa*. "You can't come to Paris and not see the *Mona Lisa*, Amy," he said. "It would be sacrilege."

Standing in front of the most famous painting in the world was a weird experience. For a start, I'd imagined an enormous picture in a wildly ornate gold frame, but the *Mona Lisa* is small, not that much bigger than a laptop screen, and the frame is pretty average. Plus, the whole painting is encased in a thick box of bulletproof plastic to protect it. Apparently, ever since *The Da Vinci Code* came out, nutters from all over the world have been threatening to shoot, burn, or steal the painting.

Security guards in sharp black suits and earpieces, who look more like nightclub bouncers than priceless-art protectors, guard the painting night and day. They watch the hordes of tourists like hawks. It's all very surreal. But it was still worth seeing—there's certainly something special about her smile.

Mills scoops the cream off the top of her hot chocolate with her finger (she's become quite the addict) and licks it. "Maybe I was wrong about Eriq. After all, he did cover for me with his parentals this morning. And he helped me find your hotel on Friday night. Maybe I should give him another chance. Shall I ring him, see if he wants to hang out with us?"

I sigh. "Mills, it's a bit late now—you're going home this afternoon. Unless you want another long-distance relationship, I'd leave it. And what about Bailey?"

Seth looks at me and then at Mills. "Is there something going on I don't know about?"

"Mills has the hots for Mr. Otis." I grin.

Mills's cheeks flare. "I do not! And don't you dare say a word to him when we get home, Seth Stone. I'd be *so* embarrassed."

"Mills, don't be so coy," I say. "Seth's hardly going to say anything. Are you, Seth?"

"'Course not. Unlike you pair, Bailey and I don't discuss our feelings 24/7. We have better things to talk about."

"Oh?" I say. "Like what?"

Seth shrugs. "Music. Movies. Cars. Gadgets. The usual."

Mills looks confused. "Gadgets?"

"Laptops, iPhones, iPods, apps"— he grins at me and winks — "*spyware.*"

I smile back at him. He's not going to let me forget that in a hurry.

Mills, who missed the joke entirely, says, "That's sad, Seth. You should both get a job at the Carphone Warehouse and be done with it. At least that way you'd earn some money from your weirdo boy obsessions."

I sit back and listen to Mills and Seth banter, lobbing playful slags at each other, like balls over a tennis net. And I feel completely, head-to-toe happy. The sun is shining, I'm in Paris with my two fave people in the whole wide world, and Seth LOVES me.

Last night, after walking back to find Clover, the three of us meandered up the Seine toward this small island in the middle of the river called Île de la Cité. It was a beautiful night, mild and bright, and the amazing stone buildings on the island were all illuminated like the Disney fairy-tale castle. Then we wandered along the streets as far as Notre Dame Cathedral, Seth holding my hand firmly the whole time. Once, when Clover wasn't looking, he pulled it to his mouth and kissed it, my skin tingling under his warm lips.

The cathedral wasn't open, but we stared up at the gargoyles and walked around the sides of the building to check out the flying buttresses that hold up the vaults (Seth insisted — he's into that kind of thing). It was magical.

Then, leaving Seth in the taxi, Clover and I got out at the Moulin Rouge and walked back to the hotel through the teeming streets curling around the Sacré Cœur. We tried on Barbie-pink cowboy hats in the tourist shops and watched people having their portraits painted and sang along to U2 songs with the buskers. I bought a lemon-colored cuddly duck for Gracie that quacks when you squeeze its tummy and a winking *Mona Lisa* fridge magnet for Dad.

Back in our room, I fell into bed in a swoon and slept more soundly than I have for a long, long time: deeply and dreamlessly. I woke up with a smile on my lips, instantly remembering Seth's promise to love me. Forever.

At one o'clock Seth and Mills have to get back and we walk to the Concorde Métro station and say our final good-byes.

"Ciao, mon amie." Mills kisses me on both cheeks then steps back.

"See you tomorrow, Amy." Seth gives me a big hug and lip smacker.

"Get a room, you two," Mills says after we've been smooching for a while. Her arms are crossed and she's tapping her foot. "We're going to miss our flight, Seth. *Vite, allez, allez!*"

I break away from Seth and laugh. "Nice French, babes, but, please, let us have our Parisian moment. Don't be such an impatient jitterbug."

Mills rolls her eyes but gives us another few minutes with no foot tapping.

After they've gone, I take the Métro back to the hotel to meet up with Mum, Monique, and Clover.

I feel *très* Parisian — if a little nervous — traveling on the Métro by myself and even negotiate a change at Charles de Gaulle Étoile station.

"Don't look so glum, French Bean," Clover says as I walk through the gates of Hôtel Unique. (She's sitting on the front steps, sunning herself.) "We'll always have Paris," she adds in a husky American accent.

"Is that from a movie?"

She smiles. "Yep. *Casablanca:* Humphrey Bogart and Ingrid Bergman. Do brush up on your classic films, Beanie. Good morning?"

I nod and smile blissfully. "The best."

She pats the step beside her and her accent turns Deep South. "Sit down on this here porch, honey child, and tell your ol' aunt Clover all about it."

♥ Chapter 28

"Paris seems like a dream," Mills says on Monday morning, pressing her head against the back of the DART seat. "I can't believe we're back to school today. So depressing. And I'm wrecked from all the traveling last night." She yawns so deeply I can see her tonsils. Which makes me yawn.

"At least your flight wasn't delayed," I point out. "I didn't get to bed till one. And Mum still made me come to school this morning. But it's better than being at home, I guess, and having to listen to the babies having a who-can-cry-the-loudest match. They really missed Mum over the weekend — Evie wouldn't let go of her at breakfast, hung around her waist like a little koala bear. Cute, but annoying for Mum — she even had to take her into the shower with her!"

Mills laughs. "Didn't her nappy get wet?"

"Sodden. But Mum said it was better than getting pooed all over. Hey, Mills, is that Bailey over there? With his back to us. It looks like him." I point to the far end of the carriage, where a boy with jet-black hair and DJ headphones is drumsticking his fingers on the window.

From the color of Mills's cheeks, I'd say it most certainly is.

"Want to join him?" I ask. I know he was avoiding me last week, but now that Mills and Seth are back, hopefully that will change.

Mills shakes her head. "We'll catch him later. Where's Seth? He's usually on this train."

I shrug. I haven't heard from him this morning, but I know he planned to come in — he wanted to catch up with Bailey. "Probably still in bed," I say. "Bet he's overslept. I'm sure he'll be in later." It is odd, though. Polly usually makes sure he gets out the door in time. I hope nothing's wrong at home. I throw him a quick text but he still hasn't replied by the time we get off the train.

He finally texts as I'm walking into the art prefab. WON'T BE IN TODAY. GOING TO THE HOSPITAL WITH

POLLY — FIRST DAY OF HER DRUG TRIAL. TALK LATER.
LOVE YOU. SETH X

Looks like I'll be suffering art all on my ownio.

At break, I sit down on the steps outside the biology lab to wait for Mills. I spot her walking along the corridor, Bailey by her side.

"Hey, Amy." She smooths down the back of her skirt and joins me on the step. Bailey lingers just behind us, playing on his mobile. It's a bit rude if you ask me — he hasn't even said hi.

"Hi, Mills," I say, before adding pointedly, "and hi, *Bailey*. Did you have a good weekend? Earth calling Bailey. Come in, Bailey." I wave my hand backward and forward in front of his face.

He looks at me, a flicker of something running across his face — irritation, annoyance, regret? It's hard to tell.

"No, not really," he says eventually. "Didn't do much. I'm glad the gang's back. And look, sorry if I was a bit off last week — things on my mind. You know how it is."

He looks genuinely sorry and a bit embarrassed, so I just say, "That's OK," and change the subject. "Seth's not coming in today. He's going to the hospital with Polly."

Bailey nods. "He told me about her being ill and all that. He's the only dude I know who actually likes his mum. But Polly seems cool."

"Have you met her?" I ask.

He nods but doesn't elaborate.

"My mum's all right most of the time," Mills says. "And Amy's mum, Sylvie, is lovely, if a bit, well, emotional."

Bailey looks surprised. "She's an emo? Is she not a bit old?"

I laugh. "As if. She's deeply uncool. ABBA and Take That are more her thing. She's permanently on the verge of a nervous breakdown — that's what Mills means."

Bailey seems a bit stumped by this. "Oh, right. So what went down in Paris? Annabelle told me that some French guy was keen on Mills. That right?"

Mills's cheeks flash red and she presses her fingers against them and looks away while I nod.

"Eriq," I say. "But she wasn't interested, were you, Mills? Only has eyes for . . ."

Mills jumps to her feet. "I've just remembered there's something I have to do. Urgently."

"I was only going to say Paris," I say to her disappearing back. "Honest."

Bailey stares after her, looking a bit confused,

then meets my eye. He's just opening his mouth to say something when the bell rings, calling us back to class. "Better motor," he says instead. "Later, Amy." He walks away, leaving me alone again.

He could have waited and walked to English with me. I sit still for a moment, thinking. When Mills was in the toilet yesterday morning in the Tuileries gardens (jeepers, was it only yesterday?), I'd told Seth that Bailey had pretty much ignored me all week. "Cut him a bit of slack, Amy," Seth said. "Without me and Mills around, he probably felt a bit vulnerable. Scared of your flashlight-in-the-eyes interrogation methods." I hit Seth on the arm but he just grinned. "Bailey's shy," he added, "and he puts up this hard shell to protect himself. But he's a good guy underneath it all, trust me. If he and Mills get together, he's going to be around a lot, so you'd better get used to him."

I do trust Seth, with all my heart, so for his sake, I'm prepared to give Bailey a second chance. But if he tramples all over Mills's heart, he'll have me to deal with.

Dad and Shelly come to see me on Tuesday after school. "We can only stay a few minutes," Dad says before he's even sat down on the sofa.

"We have to go to Mothercare in Blackrock on the

way back into town," Shelly adds, stroking Dad's arm and sitting down to his left. I perch on the arm of the sofa next to him. "People keep giving Gracie size zero-to-three-month Onesies," she continues. "It's really annoying, isn't it, Art?" She doesn't pause to let Dad answer. "She's smaller than that: size newborn. So I'm going to swap most of them."

"I wouldn't swap too many," Mum says. "She'll be out of the tiny ones pretty quickly." Shelly gives Mum a "you don't have a clue" look, but Mum just ignores her and gives Shelly a sugar-sweet smile before continuing, "But you're the expert, Shelly. What do I know about babies?"

This time Shelly gives Mum a truly evil look. Mum and Shelly don't exactly get on — they have "history," as Clover says — but I thought Gracie's arrival had changed Shelly. She seemed softer in the hospital, calmer somehow — nicer even. Clearly not. She seems back to her old annoying self today: shopping obsessed, snappy, and defensive. Maybe Shelly's bored of Gracie already. Poor Gracie; she's still so tiny — for her sake, I hope not.

Dad coughs and looks a bit nervous. I give him what I hope is a reassuring smile while Shelly twitters on. "And I've *finally* found a drugstore that sells the Naturally Beautiful organic baby range.

It's from California and all the stars use it on their little ones. That's why we're out this direction in the first place. Mum's in the hospital with Gracie, and I made Art take the afternoon off to drive me. I get so terribly lost in the suburbs. Art thought we might as well visit while we're so far out of town."

Mum and I exchange a look; Glenageary is hardly the sticks. And I'd thought they'd come especially to see *me*. I'm hurt, but I try not to show it.

"When's Gracie coming out of the hospital, Dad?" I ask.

He looks confused. "Didn't I tell you? Friday, all being well."

I shake my head. "No. And I tried calling you from Paris to find out how she was doing, but your phone went straight to messages and you never called back."

"Sorry," he says. "The doctors still have a few more tests to run, but if they're happy with her breathing and her eating, and the hole in her heart stays firmly closed, then it's good-bye, Parnell Street, thank the Lord."

"That must be a relief," Mum says. "Are you going to have her christened while Pauline's still here or wait awhile?"

"There's no rush," Shelly says, even though Mum directed the question at Dad. "Mum's going to stay till Christmas. And in the New Year we'll see what happens."

"Christmas?" Dad splutters. "When were you thinking of telling me that, Shelly? That's months away!"

Shelly pats Dad's hand. "I know. But it might take months to find the right nanny for our little girl. And Mum's offered to help out until then."

"Are you going back to work after Christmas, Shelly?" Mum asks.

"Work?" Shelly says. "Gosh, no. My Gracie needs me at home."

Mum looks confused. "I thought you just said you were hiring a nanny."

"We are. I can't look after Gracie all by myself, now, can I? How would I go shopping or to the hairdresser's?" Her eyes go all wide and owl-like.

Mum opens her mouth to say something, but Dad interrupts. "We'd better get going, Shelly." He turns to me. "All being well, you can come over next weekend and spend a whole day with your baby sister. Would you like that?"

"Yes. Thanks, Dad." Then something occurs to me. "But you're not going golfing, are you?" Being left alone with Shelly *and* Pauline would be a fate worse than death.

He smiles. "Absolutely not. No golf for a long time — and that's a promise." He leans over and gives me a hug.

It's only after Dad and Shelly have left that I remember Dad and Gracie's presents from Paris. I run upstairs to grab them, but by the time I get back downstairs again, Dad has already pulled away. I squeeze the little duck in my hand, making it quack. I feel hollow all of a sudden: teary.

When I turn around, Mum is standing in the doorway to the living room.

"I forgot to give Dad his present from Paris," I say. "If he'd asked me about the trip, I would have remembered. But he didn't even mention it."

She sighs, her eyes soft. "They're both a bit baby obsessed at the moment, Amy, but it'll pass. Are you OK? You look a little pale."

I don't trust myself to say anything without bursting into tears, so I just shrug.

Mum puts her hand on my forehead. "You are a little hot. Hope you didn't catch one of those funny foreign flus in Paris. You'd better hop into bed and rest."

We go back upstairs. She pulls back the duvet and I flick off my runners and crawl under gratefully, the duvet cool and heavy on my skin. As soon as she's left the room, I finally allow myself to cry.

♥ Chapter 29

That night I still feel low, so I ring Mills for a chat.

"Hi, Amy. How funny—I was about to ring you. I'm so worried about Bailey."

"He's being a bit weird all right."

"I know. Do you think it's because of Eriq?"

"Eriq?" (What is she on about?)

"Maybe Annabelle told him more than he's letting on? Do you think he's annoyed with me? Or upset? Or maybe he's . . ."

I listen to her obsess about Bailey and what he's thinking for a few more minutes. To be honest, I've had quite enough of her boy drama-ramas to last a whole month. I know it's ungracious—she's a good friend and always listens to my Seth woes—but I can't help how I feel.

Midflow, I say, "I'm really sorry, Mills, but Evie's crying and Mum's downstairs. I'd better check on her. See you tomorrow." And I click off the phone. It's a total lie but I just can't take any more. Then I punch in Clover's number. No answer. I throw my phone onto my bed in disgust.

I'm bored rigid in my room, so I wander into the hall looking for distraction. Mum and Dave's door is open and I peep inside. Mum's standing in the middle of the floor, staring at our bridesmaids' dresses, which are hanging in their thin plastic see-through wrappers on the front of her wardrobe.

"Mum?" I say, and she turns around.

She looks miserable. Her eyes are wet and she wipes them with her fingers.

"What's wrong?" I ask.

She sniffs. "Nothing. I'm fine."

"You don't look fine. You look terrible. Shall I call Dave?"

"No!" Mum's face crumples and she starts crying again.

"Sit down, Mum." I pull her by the arm toward the bed and she sits on the edge and stares down at her hands, now clasped in her lap.

"What's wrong?" I ask again.

"It's nothing, Amy, honestly. I'm just having a bit of a wobble."

"Is it the dresses? Have you changed your mind — is that it?"

"No, I love the dresses."

"What, then?"

She sighs. "It's the whole wedding thing. I think I'm having second thoughts."

I sit down beside her. "I know Clover's going a bit overboard with the whole matching flowers and cupcakes —"

"It's not the flowers or the cupcakes; it's the idea of standing in front of everyone, again, and taking more wedding vows. It terrifies me."

OK, this is not good, not good at all. "You don't want to get married at all?" I ask.

"I'm not sure."

"Why? You love Dave, don't you?"

She nods. "It's not that."

"What is it, then?"

"Amy, I shouldn't be talking to you about all this. I'm sorry. It's wrong of me to involve you."

"Mum, I hate to point it out, but this affects me too. And Alex and Evie. All of us. And before Dave came along, you talked to me about a lot of things, remember? About Dad and everything."

Mum winces. "Well, I shouldn't have. It wasn't right."

"Mum, tell me what's wrong, please? Maybe I can help."

"That's very sweet of you, Amy, but I don't think—"

"Stop treating me like a child," I say strongly. "I'm thirteen, not four. At the very least, I can listen."

Tears are running down Mum's face and she says nothing for a while, then eventually nods again. "Sorry. You're right. I just feel like I burden you with too much, you know, and it's not fair. Mills doesn't have to deal with half the stuff you do."

"OK, maybe Mills doesn't, but Seth's mum has cancer," I point out. "Everyone has their own problems to deal with. At least we *can* talk, Mum. Some people hate their mothers." I think of Sophie's mum, Mrs. Piggott, who's a witch. She even accused me of stealing her pearl necklace at the end-of-term party in her house.

"Yes, we can." Mum rubs her eyes with her hands. "OK, if you really want to know, I'm worried that things will change between me and Dave after we're married. That he'll start to feel even more tied down. He's only thirty-two, and before we met, he was this cool musician, playing gigs all over Ireland. Now he's a nurse and working all hours to make enough money to pay bills. Maybe getting married will put even more pressure on him and make things worse. I know I'll have a job soon, but still . . ."

She pauses for a second, blows out her breath, and then says, "And in Paris, I had such fun, drinking cocktails and hanging out with Monique and you guys. I felt more alive than I have in years. I felt like *me:* Sylvie Wildgust. Not Mrs. Green or Mrs. Marcus — just me. And for the first time in a long time, it felt good being me. And I don't know if I'm ready to give that up yet. I know it's selfish, but it's just how I feel." She looks at me, her eyes sad. "Does that sound terrible?"

"No, not at all. Mum, if you're not ready, then you're not ready. Have you told Dave any of this?"

She shakes her head. "I can't. He'll be so upset. After plucking up the courage to ask me like that, in front of all those people, I can't back out now." (Last summer, Clover and I helped Dave plan his proposal. We drew a huge heart in the sand on Inchydoney Beach and Dave stood in it and asked Mum to marry him. It was very romantic.)

"Maybe it's just nerves," I say. "All brides get prewedding jitters — everyone knows that. I bet you were nervous walking up the aisle toward Dad."

Mum snorts. "Only that he'd do a runner to Toronto and leave me jilted. He always wanted to emigrate to Canada, but I refused to go with him — didn't want to leave Monique and Gran and Gramps and Clover behind. Perhaps things would have been different if I'd agreed. . . ."

"There's no point worrying about it now," I say gently. "You know what they say: 'No regrets, they don't work.'" (I'm quoting an old Robbie Williams song at her, but she doesn't seem to notice.)

"Sorry," she says again, pressing her fingertips against her eyes. "Maybe I am overreacting and maybe you're right: it's just nerves."

Mum, a bigger drama queen than Mills, over-reacting — never! I try not to smile.

"So the wedding's still on?" I ask.

"I guess so. I'm probably just a bit out of sorts with all the traveling and everything."

"Shall I make you a cup of tea?"

She nods. "Thanks, Amy. The color's back in your face. Are you feeling better?"

"Yes. I think I was just tired."

"In that case, have you done your homework?"

I sigh. Mum seems to have this built-in default "homework" mechanism. After me listening to her wedding dilemmas and being so nice to her, you'd think she'd let me off for one night, but oh, no. Typical!

"Nearly," I lie. "I'll bring the tea up to you, then get straight back to my desk."

"You're a good girl, Amy. I don't deserve you." Her eyes well up again, so I murmur, "Tea," and flee.

In the kitchen, I ring Clover again. And this time she answers.

"Clover, help!" I hiss into my mobile while waiting for the kettle to boil. "Mum's having second thoughts about the wedding."

"She can't be. I've put acres of work into it already. And there's no way those fab bridesmaids' dresses are going to waste. I'll be right over to firefight, Beanie."

Whatever Clover says to Mum seems to do the trick. Mum potters off to bed early with a copy of the latest edition of *Irish Bride*, courtesy of her fairy godsister.

"I heard she was nervous before her first wedding," Clover says, collapsing on the sofa beside me. "But nowhere near this bad."

"You don't think she'll call the whole thing off, do you?" I pick at the skin around my thumb. This whole wedding-jitters business is making *me* very nervous.

"Nah, give her a few days, she'll be all wedding systems go. How's everything else? Sylvie told me Gracie's coming home on Friday. Pretty cool, eh?"

"Suppose." I shrug.

"Thought you'd be cow jumps over the moon excited, Beanie. What's up?"

"It's Dad. He was over earlier — but only because he was *shopping* in Blackrock for Gracie. He doesn't seem to care about me anymore. He didn't even ask me or Mum how Paris went, and he's asked Pauline to stay until Christmas to help with Gracie. Bang goes the big-sister babysitting!" (OK, that last bit is a slight exaggeration, but I'm so fed up I just don't care.)

Clover says nothing for a few seconds, then starts to talk, a slightly dreamy look in her eyes. "I was only four when you were born. The first few weeks Sylvie went baby mad — every word out of her mouth was *Amy this; Amy that*. It drove me crazy."

I look at her in surprise. "You remember being four?"

"Parts of it. Anyway, when you were only a week old, I threw some of your cuddly toys down the loo and hid your blankie. Mum was so cross she slapped me across the back of the legs. The following week I woke you up by poking you in the eye. Hard. It left a yellow bruise on your eyelid and everything. You yelled for hours, and I wasn't allowed near you on my own after that."

Clover runs her hand over my cheek. "I guess I thought Sylvie had forgotten all about me. Which she had. But it didn't last long. It's natural to feel a bit left out, and compared to me, you're behaving like an angel. Art will soon snap out of it, you'll see. If he doesn't, he'll have me to deal with. Do you want me to talk to him for you?"

"Thanks, Clover." I rub my head on her shoulder. "You're the best. But this is one problem I need to deal with myself."

"I understand." Then she grins and puts out her hand. "That will be fifty euro for the counseling session. But I'll happily take my payment in chocolate. Anything hidden in Dave's drawer?"

I smile back. Clover always manages to make me feel better.

Mum seems fine the following morning until a Concern ad about sick African babies comes on the telly, and then she's off again, her eyes swimming with tears. "Those poor children," she wails. "I just can't bear it. Amy, switch it off, quick!"

I hand her some paper towels. "Take it easy today, Mum."

She gives me a weak smile. "The sooner I get back to work, the better. Take my mind off . . . "—she pauses—"everything."

"You all right, Sylvie?" Dave walks into the kitchen, rubbing his sleepy eyes.

"Concern ad," Mum says with a sniff.

He nods. He's used to Mum's sensitivities. I wish he'd stayed upstairs, though. He's wearing a crumpled Killers T-shirt over checked boxers. I hate seeing him in his underwear—*soooo* embarrassing.

He notices my wince and pulls his T-shirt down a bit. "Sorry. Thought you'd be off to school by now, Amy."

"Just leaving." I grab my bag and vamoose.

♥ Chapter 30

Dad rings me on Thursday evening. "What are you up to, Amy? Can you talk?"

"Only homework, so definitely yes."

He laughs. "Don't let your mother hear you. Listen, we're thinking of having a welcome-home party for Gracie on Saturday afternoon. Bit of food, champagne, that kind of thing. You free? And do you think your mum and Dave would like to come?"

"Count me in. And I'm sure they'd love to. What about Clover?"

"Of course. She did an amazing job getting Shelly to the hospital so quickly. Quite the mad dash, eh?"

It's the first time Dad's mentioned the role Clover played in the Parnell Street escapade. I wait, expecting him to acknowledge *my* part, but he just adds, "Gramps too if he's around."

"I'll tell them," I say, trying to keep a sigh out of my voice.

"Pauline's dying to meet Gramps," he says, oblivious.

"Really? I'd better warn him about her in that case."

Dad chuckles. "She's off in Dundrum buying a new outfit for the party as we speak; took Shelly with her. The woman seems to spend half her life shopping. But with Gracie coming out of the hospital tomorrow, I guess it's the last chance Shelly will get for a while. She wants to buy some sort of special baby blanket with Velcro on it and another thermometer for Gracie's room. She doesn't trust the one we have already."

Is he kidding? Shelly will probably spend 99 percent of her time in Dundrum, shopping and lunching — they don't call posh new mums Yummy Drummies for nothing, and retail therapy seems to be in the Lame blood. He'll learn soon enough, though, so I say nothing.

"They wouldn't let me go with them," he continues. "Well, Pauline wouldn't. Shelly wouldn't be that mean." (I have to stop myself from snorting.) "I'm a bit sick of being left out, to be honest," he goes on. "I even took some time off this morning to help bathe Gracie, but Pauline wouldn't let me near her, insisted she'd help Shelly and sent me packing. And it's not the first time. Last week . . ."

And as I listen to Dad's litany of Pauline-related woes and hear how abandoned he's feeling, I get more and more irritated. He really is clueless. How can he not realize he's doing exactly the same thing to me? I have to do something.

Finally, I interrupt his moans. "Dad, stop a minute. Look, can you come over? I need to talk to you."

"Is everything all right, Amy?"

"Not really, but we need to talk about it in person."

"OK. Nothing too serious, I hope?"

I sigh. "Just come over, Dad, please."

"Have you eaten?"

"No, why?"

"I was about to order a pizza. If you can wait forty minutes or so, I'll come by and get you: how about Milano's in Dun Laoghaire?"

"Sounds like a plan. See you then." I click off my mobile, my stomach already a butterfly farm of nerves. Talking to Dad isn't going to be easy, but I just feel that if I don't do it now, I might never do it.

Here's the thing (I've been thinking about it

a lot): Dad ignoring me (unless he wants to moan about Pauline), I can handle, but I don't want me and Gracie to have the kind of relationship Sophie Piggott has with her half-sister, who she only sees at Christmas and birthdays. I want to be a proper part of Gracie's life — someone she can rely on. With Shelly for a mum, and Dad the way he is, she genuinely needs me. If it weren't for Clover, I don't know how I'd cope. I want to be Gracie's Clover. And personally, I think that's worth fighting for.

I'm sitting in the passenger seat of Dad's car, picking at the skin around my thumb, too nervous to say anything yet. Dad seems happy enough to concentrate on his driving, tapping his fingers on the wheel in time to an ancient Phil Collins song about living separate lives. I try to block it out.

We drive past Dun Laoghaire Park and swing a left toward Milano's, Dublin Bay stretching out in front of us, the gray blue of a whale's back. There are dark clouds in the sky and it looks like it's about to rain. Dad parks outside the Royal Saint George Yacht Club, and the minute the engine's off, he starts moaning again. "Remember I was telling you about Pauline not letting me bathe Gracie?" (Oh, no, here we go.)

"She won't let me change her nappy either. Makes me sit and watch while she does it."

"Dad, you hate changing nappies."

He sniffs. "That's not the point. Gracie's my daughter and Pauline won't let me near her most of the time." He sits back in his seat and crosses his arms huffily. "My own daughter. I feel so left out."

I stare at him. "Really? *You* feel left out?" I load my voice with sarcasm, but he doesn't seem to notice.

He nods. "I wish Pauline would just go off back to Portugal and leave me and Shelly alone. We don't need her or anyone else's help at the moment. Me, Shelly, Gracie — they're the only people I want in the house. Just the three of us." He realizes the second it's out what he's just said, but it's too late.

My heart starts pounding in my chest and I'm so upset I can hardly breathe. Before I know what I'm doing, my hand is on the door handle and I'm out of the car and sprinting past the yacht club toward the East Pier.

"Amy, wait!"

I hear the bang of a car door, then Dad's feet pounding the pavement behind me. I pick up speed. When I reach the top of the pier, a stitch is building in my stomach but I keep running.

Dad is just behind me. "Amy!" He grabs my arm. "Stop!"

I give in to him. It's a relief, to be honest. I bend over and puff and pant a little, trying to relieve the stitch. Dad's out of breath too.

"Amy, I'm so sorry. I wasn't thinking," he says.

I stay low, putting my hand over my face to shield the tears that are now splattering onto the polished concrete surface.

"Ah, baby. Come here." He pulls me up and puts both arms around my back, hugging me tight.

I only let him hold me for a split second, then pull away.

"I'm so sorry," he says again. "I know you're upset by what I said, but please, don't ever run away from me like that again. Talk to me; tell me how you're feeling."

I turn around and face him. "I would if I could get a word in, Dad. It's all *me, me, me* with you these days. *Nasty Pauline is picking on me.* Well, boo, hoo. You need to listen to yourself!"

"Amy!" He looks genuinely shocked that I'm so angry with him. "Have I really been all that self-absorbed?" he asks.

"Yes! You never even asked me about Paris," I say, my eyes sparkling. "You say *you* feel left out.

Well, I haven't seen my sister for nearly two weeks 'cos you're all too busy shopping to bother about me. Gracie doesn't need all that stuff you're buying her. She just needs you both to love her. And pay attention to her. And let her see the other people who love her—" I break off, a lump forming in my throat. "As for saying the only people you want in the house are you, Shelly, and Gracie, how do you think that makes *me* feel?"

Dad sighs and shakes his head. "I know how it must have sounded. I wasn't thinking, Amy. Of course, I meant the four of us. You, me, Shelly, and Gracie."

"That's just it: you don't think. You say these things all the time."

"I'm sorry. I'll try not to be so insensitive. And you'll see Gracie every second weekend, I promise."

He's still not getting it. "That's not what I mean. It's not about the visits. I know I don't live with you guys, so I'm not going to see Gracie every day, but I still want to be a *proper* sister to her, not just someone she sees every second weekend. She needs me, Dad. Don't you understand?"

Dad looks a little awkward. (He's always hated emotional confrontations. You should hear Mum on the subject.) "You're right," he says eventually. "She does need you. And so do I. I'll try to be a better dad, honest." He smiles at me and then pulls me into a hug.

I sigh into his shirt, give in, and hug him back. (It's impossible to be cross with Dad for long.) After a moment, I pull away. "Look, there's another reason I wanted to see you. I have presents for you and Gracie. From Paris. They're in the car."

"You shouldn't be spending your money on us."

"But you're my dad, and Gracie's my sister — not my *half*-sister, like you said. My proper, 100 percent sister." My God, do I have to drill it into his big, thick skull?!

He looks embarrassed. "I only called her that because I thought that's what you wanted."

"What *I* wanted?"

He nods. "When I first told you you'd have a new brother or sister, way back in the spring, you said *half*-brother or *half*-sister, remember?"

And it comes back to me. *Siúcra*, he's right. "I didn't mean it. I was upset."

"I know. And I want you in Gracie's life, honestly I do. But she's only a couple of weeks old, Amy. She can't even talk yet."

"Dad, I know you're not really all that keen on babies —"

"That's just not true," he blusters.

I look at him, my eyebrow cocked.

"OK, I admit I find them hard work. Once they can talk and kick a ball around, they get a lot more interesting. But, for God's sake, don't tell Shelly or Pauline that."

"As if. But *I* love babies. You know I love babies. Watching them, holding their tiny hands, smelling their necks — everything about them. You start bonding with babies from day one, Dad. You can't just plonk yourself into their lives as soon as they're potty trained; you have to be there for the long haul, changing nappies, bathing them, rocking them to sleep, singing to them — not Phil Collins, obviously, songs babies like, nursery rhymes and lullabies."

He smiles. "Nothing wrong with Phil Collins. He's the man."

I roll my eyes. (When it comes to music, Dad is clearly delusional.) "And, Dad, *you* have to start getting more involved with looking after Gracie. Sounds to me like you're standing back and *letting* Pauline take over. Tell her how you feel; ask her to show you how to bathe Gracie properly and change her nappies. Prove you can do it on your own. Tell her you want to bond with Gracie. Be more assertive."

Dad's staring at me. "Amy Green, how do you know so much about what makes people tick?"

I shrug. "Some of it's from Clover, but I'm interested in people — I watch them, ask a lot of questions. I listen to them."

Dad laughs. "I guess you do." He looks at me, really looks at me, his eyes soft and a little sad. "I don't deserve you, Amy. I'm a terrible dad."

"You're not that bad," I say, nudging him with my shoulder. (He is pretty useless sometimes, but he's still my dad.) "I'll be your starter daughter. You can learn about being a dad using me, make all the mistakes you like, but try to get it right with Gracie, OK?"

He nods, his eyes glistening with tears. "I'm so sorry, Amy." Uh-oh, I'm used to Mama Meltdown, but Papa Meltdown is a new one on me.

"Dad, it was a joke! Please don't go all mushy on me. I get enough of that at home."

He wipes his eyes with his knuckles and smiles gently. "From now on, things are going to change; you can see Gracie whenever you like, I promise. And if Shelly and Pauline have anything to say about it, they'll have me to deal with. And we're going to have a regular pizza night, just you and me."

I give him a hug and then my stomach rumbles like an active volcano. "Speaking of food," I say, drawing away. "I'm starving. Can we eat now?"

All this drama has made me extra hungry.

♥ Chapter 31

By lunchtime on Saturday, Pauline's in full swing, waving her empty champagne flute around like a sword and yelling, "More glue, Vicar?"—whatever that means. She's been flirting with Gramps all afternoon, snaking around him in a tiered white country-and-western skirt—which Clover is not finding amusing.

We're all at Gracie's homecoming party: me, Gramps, Clover, Mum, Dave, Evie, and Alex. Mum spent the first ten minutes studying the elaborate curtain swags, the tassels on the bottom of the vast cream sofa, the perfect white walls, the delicate angel ornaments on glass shelves—Shelly has a thing about angels—and smiling to herself.

When I asked Clover why Mum was looking so happy, she said, "I think she's imagining Little Miss

Perky's palace once Gracie starts smashing the angels and scribbling on the walls."

Dad refills Pauline's glass with champagne and taps his own flute with his wedding ring. *Clink, clink, clink.*

We all hush.

"I'd like to thank you all for coming here today to celebrate Gracie's homecoming," he says.

Alex burps loudly and everyone laughs, except for Pauline, who scowls at him. At least I think it's a scowl; her forehead is so rigid it's hard to tell. It's wasted on Alex, anyway. He just waves at her gleefully with his podgy hand.

Dad raises his glass. "To Gracie Amber Green. *Sláinte.*"

"Otherwise known as Gracie Traffic Lights," Clover whispers in my ear as she taps her glass against mine.

I chuckle. "Shush, Clover!"

Pauline glares at *us* this time.

"Ooh, I think I saw a wrinkle," Clover hisses. "If your woman is staying in Dublin till Christmas, she'd better start checking out the local Botox clinics."

I put my hand over my mouth to stifle my giggles as Dad continues, "I'd also like to thank Gracie's big sister, Amy, for all her help. Without Amy, Gracie may not have made it safely into this world, and for that, both Shelly and I are eternally grateful. And thanks to Clover too, for her rally driving."

Everyone laughs.

"So," Dad goes on, "we'd like to ask Amy to be Gracie's godmother and to keep watching over her as she grows up. Like Gracie's guardian angel."

Before I get the chance to say anything, Pauline clears her throat loudly. "That's a bit unconventional — a half-sister as a godmother."

"So's dressing like a cowboy unless it's a costume party," Clover says, quick as a flash. "But we've all been too polite to mention it. That's quite an outfit." (Pauline's frilly skirt, matching waistcoat, and red-checked shirt are quite something all right.)

Pauline gulps, opening and closing her mouth like a guppy fish. "Well, I never," she says.

"Clover!" Mum says in a warning tone, but from the spark in her eye I can tell she thinks it's hilarious.

All the while, Pauline keeps on glaring at Clover, her eyes screwed tight. (Oops, I think Clover's made an enemy.) But I don't plan to let Pauline spoil my big moment. I'm going to be Gracie's godmother!

I lock eyes with Dad and beam. "Thanks, Dad. I'd love to be Gracie's godmother. Any excuse to shop. She'll need sister *and* godmother presents now. Yeah!" I clasp my hands into fists and wave them in the air.

Everyone laughs again.

"I'm hoping you'll look out for Gracie the way Clover looks out for you," Dad adds. OK, finally, FINALLY, he gets it. My heart feels as light as a hummingbird.

"Aah," Mum says. "That's so sweet."

And for once in her life, Clover is lost for words. I grin at her, and she smiles back and winks.

"And now, a toast to Godmother Amy." Dad holds up his glass again. "And just think, the next time we all drink this stuff will be at Sylvie and Dave's wedding. *Sláinte*."

"To Godmother Amy," everyone says, clinking glasses. "*Sláinte*."

Mum's back has stiffened at the mention of her wedding, but no one's noticed except me and Clover. Dave looks delighted. He grins and puts his arms around Mum from behind. She wasn't expecting it and her glass wobbles, spilling champagne down her wrap dress.

"Sorry," Dave says.

Mum dabs at it with a napkin. "It's patterned. Won't show a stain."

Seconds later there's a smashing noise in the kitchen and Alex runs back in, crying, his T-shirt and arms dripping wet.

Clover grabs one of his arms as he dashes past and licks it. "More spilled champagne." She grins at Alex. "Starting early, mini-man."

Pauline and Shelly gasp and disappear into the kitchen.

Alex's cries have startled Evie, who in turn sets Gracie off. Mum and Dave decide it's a good time to leave, but Alex is having none of it. He collapses on the floor and windmills his arms and legs in a full-blown toddler tantrum.

As we watch the mayhem from the sidelines, Clover says, "I think what Sylvie needs is a cracking hen night. Banish all those prewedding jitters. What d'ya think, Godmother Beanie?"

"*Absolument.* How about a really posh restaurant? Or a pampering day at a spa?"

Clover's eyes glitter. "I was thinking something a little more unusual. What's your mum's favorite city in the whole entire universe?"

I don't even have to think about it. "New York. But wouldn't that be a bit expensive? Mum's worried about the cost of the wedding as it is."

"Ah, but what if we bring New York to Dublin,

complete with a tour to rival the *Sex and the City* one and our very own Tiffany's experience?"

"We could have a picnic in Saint Stephen's Green Park instead of Central Park!" I suggest.

Clover claps her hands together. "Good thinking, Beanie. And we don't have an Empire State Building, but we do have . . ."

I grin from ear to ear. I love it when a plan comes together.

♥ Chapter 32

The following afternoon my mobile rings.

"Amy, what are you doing right now?" It's Shelly and she sounds frantic. Gracie is crying in the background, and from the little hiccuppy and gulpy sounds, I'd say she's been at it for quite some time. I instantly start to worry. It can't be good for a baby with a heart condition to cry so much, can it?

"Why?" I ask, irritated. She should be looking after Gracie, not ringing me. Besides, Seth's coming over soon, and I'm currently trying to find the right casual-yet-cool outfit. I know in his *Goss* article Brains claimed that boys don't really care about clothes, but for a guy, Seth is pretty observant. I'm really looking forward to seeing him. I didn't see him at all yesterday and I want to find out how Polly's treatment is going. He doesn't like talking about it at school, and whenever I ask him on the phone, he just says, "Fine," and changes the subject.

"Gracie won't stop crying," Shelly wails.

"Where's Dad?"

"Golf." She spits it out, like a dirty word.

"Where?"

"Portmarnock. And he's not answering his phone. What am I going to do?"

It's pretty off of Dad to abandon Shelly — I can't believe he's golfing again when Gracie's only just home, especially when he promised he wouldn't be playing for a while. Typical Dad. And where is the oh-so-attentive Granny Pauline?

"And your mum?" I ask.

"At a spa in Enniskerry. Getting some, um . . . urgent treatments. She's not answering her phone either."

Which leaves — me. *Holy Moly*, as Mills would say. But when it comes to babies, I do have a lot of experience — Evie's a right little banshee when she gets going.

"Have you tried a pacifier?" I ask.

"She just spits it out."

"OK, what about rocking her?"

"I'm not stupid, Amy."

I'm tempted to say, "Really?" but I don't. Gracie is my little sister, not to mention my godchild now; it's my duty to help. And I do feel a bit sorry for Shelly, even if she is back to her old self — she sounds completely wired.

"What about walking her?" I suggest.

"Outside?"

(Now, if that's not a silly question, I don't know what is.) "Yes, outside."

"Amy, I'm so tired I can barely stand, let alone walk. She didn't sleep a wink last night. I can't stand much more of this." She lets out a high-pitched scream, like a cat being strangled. "Should I ring the hospital, ask their advice?"

I can't believe Dad left Shelly in this state, although I have a niggling feeling that her fragile state is part of the reason he's on the green today. I can forgive Dad — somehow I always do — but how could Pauline leave her?

"Drive down to Enniskerry," I say, "hand Gracie over to your mum, and take a nap in the car."

"If I knew the name of the spa, I might actually do that," Shelly cries. "I neeeeed sleeeep!"

"I've got it! Mum used to make Dave drive around the neighborhood with Evie in her car seat to get her to drop off. Have you tried that? You could just drive around Phoenix Park or visit a friend or something."

"Do you think it will work?" Her voice sounds painfully hopeful.

"Definitely."

"Then I'll do it. See you soon, Amy."

I'm just topping up my lip gloss when the doorbell rings. I bound down the stairs in my black skinny jeans, sparkly silver Converse (Clover just bought herself a ruby-slippers pair and gifted her old ones to me), black-and-white-striped tee, and one of Dave's old black leather waistcoats.

I swing open the door. "Hey, Seth," I begin, but it's not Seth — it's Shelly!

OK, when she said, "See you soon," I didn't realize she meant *that* soon. She looks like she's been in some sort of natural disaster — black roots are sniggling down her hair, she's not wearing any makeup and her skin is pale and blotchy, and though I hate to say it, she's not exactly fragrant smelling either. But most frightening of all, I can see a flabby muffin top flopping over the waistband of her purple Juicy tracky bottoms.

"Gracie's in the car," she says. "You were right; she finally nodded off. Amy, I partly came over because

I never got to say thank you in person at the party. For getting me to the hospital and everything. Here, this is for you. Art was supposed to give it to you yesterday, only with all the commotion, he forgot." She pulls an O2 bag out of her enormous designer changing bag.

I peer inside, fish out a silky smooth black box, and open it. A brand-spanking-new iPhone in glossy, gorgeous white.

I grin at her. "Thanks, Shelly. I've wanted one for ages."

"We both might have died if it weren't for you," she says, and her eyes well up. Then she yawns so deeply I'm almost sucked into her mouth. "Would you get Gracie for me? Please, Amy? I think I've done something to my back." She hands me the car keys.

"I'm kind of busy, Shelly. . . ." I say, but she just lumbers past me, shoulders lopsided with the huge changing bag she's carrying, and walks into the living room.

I sigh. I guess she did just give me an iPhone, so I go outside to fetch Gracie. She's fast asleep in her little car seat. I unclick it carefully and carry the whole thing inside. Putting it down gently on the hall floor, I stand back to stare at her little face.

Gracie's fluffy mop of strawberry-blond hair is welded to her pink cheeks with dried tears. She's still so tiny I catch my breath just looking at her.

Just then the doorbell rings again. *DING DONG.*

Her eyes flicker and then open. Oops. She opens her rosebud mouth and starts to wail.

"Shelly," I call into the living room. "Shelly!" Nothing.

I open the door. This time it is Seth. He walks in and stares at Gracie, his eyes hidden behind dark aviator glasses. "Has Evie shrunk?"

I chuckle. "It's Gracie. Shelly couldn't get her to sleep and drove over here." I make a face. "Sorry." Then turning, I shout across the hall again, "Shelly!" Still nothing.

"Just a second," I tell him and walk into the living room. I find Shelly stretched out on the sofa, eyes closed.

I shake her shoulder. "Shelly, Gracie is crying again."

She peels open one eye then the other. "I think I'm going to die if I don't get some sleep."

Be charitable, Amy, I tell myself. "Why don't I take her for a walk?" I hear my nicer self saying. "You can have a nap on the sofa."

"Really? I'd kill for a nap. That's so sweet of you, Amy. And, and . . ." She breaks off. "Sorry, I wanted to say something else, but I've forgotten."

"Baby brain," I say. "Mum used to forget everything when the babies were small. It's your body's way of slowing you down, apparently."

"Baby brain," Shelly repeats, then yawns again, her eyelids fluttering.

"Go to sleep," I say gently, putting a blanket over her waist and legs. "Gracie will be safe with me."

Shelly's snoring gently before I'm even out of the room. I go back out into the hall. Seth is bent over Gracie's seat, rocking it with his hand.

"Not exactly a contented baba, is she?" he says.

"No. Look, I'm really sorry: I told Shelly I'd take her for a walk. She's not fit to drive, and I don't want her crashing with Gracie in the car. Guess I'm stuck babysitting — for a change."

He shrugs. "'S OK. Sun's out. I'll come with you."

We walk down Silchester Road toward the shops, Gracie strapped to my chest in Evie's tie-dyed baby sling. (Shelly, genius that she is, didn't think to pack Gracie's pram.) She seems to like the sling. She feels warm and is snuggled against me like a little bush baby. She's found her thumb and is sucking away. And hallelujah, she's finally stopped crying!

At the shop, we buy ice creams and walk along the seafront.

"So how's Polly doing?" I ask, after I've munched the last of my Iceberger.

"Good. The drugs they're giving her are pretty strong, but so far she hasn't had too many side effects. She's tired and she's having hot flushes, but that's pretty normal, apparently. Dr. Shine is pleased with her first week's progress, and Dave seems to think everything's looking pretty positive so far."

"That's fab news, Seth. You must be relieved."

"No kidding."

I stop to adjust the straps on the sling. For a wee thing, Gracie is surprisingly heavy.

"You OK?" Seth asks. "I can take her if you like."

I stare at him in surprise. "You'd seriously do that?"

"Sure, why not? Babies are the latest fashion accessory, didn't you know?"

I smile. This I have to see. I stop and carefully untie the straps, supporting Gracie's little body with my other hand. Then Seth holds her carefully against his chest while I secure the straps around his neck. I stand back and stare at him. He looks so cute. And I can't help it: I start laughing.

"What's so funny?" he asks.

"The shades. If you weren't so fit, you'd look exactly like that dude from *The Hangover*."

Seth smiles. "As long as no one from school sees us, I don't care. Imagine the rumors. The D4s would have a field day. Speaking of school, what's Mills up to today?"

"Don't know. Nothing involving the male of the species, I hope. She has more boy trouble than anyone I know! I wish she'd just keep away from them; it would make my life a whole heap easier."

"Even Bailey Otis?" He grins. "He hasn't said anything but I think he likes her."

"*Especially* Bailey Otis. He's far too moody and secretive."

"Amy! Give the guy a break. There's nothing wrong with having a few secrets."

Gracie starts to whimper, and as I reach over and stroke her downy hair, she twists her head and tries to suck on my finger.

"I think she's hungry," I say. "Better get her back to Sleeping Beauty."

By the time we reach the front door, Gracie is slumbering again — typical. Before I take my keys out, I turn to Seth.

"Do *you* have secrets?" I ask him.

His sky-blue eyes are warm and kind. "Not from you, Amy. Never from you."

And you know something, I believe him. I look at him, Gracie still strapped across his muscular chest, and my heart soars. I'm the luckiest girl in Ireland.

Acknowledgments

This is the bit where I get to thank my long-suffering friends and family. So: to my mum and dad, my little sisters, Kate and Emma, and Richard, the brother that no one believes exists (he lives in Australia!) — I thank you yet again. For all the babysitting and general hand-holding, and for taking it so well when I won't let you in the front door 'cos I'm in the middle of a vital Amy and Clover scene — that would be you, Mum!

To Ben and the kids — thanks for keeping out of my way at vital moments (see above). Sorry for putting my hand up like a traffic warden and saying, "Don't talk to me." *Très* rude, I know, but what can I say? Writers are strange beasts. And to Sam especially, who was amazingly helpful with Brains's article on boys. I won't tell you which bits are his — he'd kill me.

I have to thank Nicky and Tanya and Andrew, 'cos I always thank them, and if I don't, people might think we've had some sort of dramatic fall-out, which we most certainly have not. I've given each one of them countless reasons to dump me, but they're still hanging in there. Bless! And here's to more girls' trips to far-flung lands.

And a big shout-out to my lovely writerly friend and honesty gauge Martina Devlin, who knows far more big words than anyone I've ever met and doesn't laugh at me when I ask her daft grammatical questions.

Big thanks also to my fellow Your Wildest Dreams Tour writers Judi Curtin and Sophia Bennett, for all their enthusiasm and funny e-mails. And to Oisin McGann and David Maybury, for all the informative book e-mails and blog entries. You are stars, gentlemen! And to my agents, Philippa Milnes-Smith and Peta Nightingale, who have both taken such good care of me over the past year.

To the gang at Walker — what can I say? For taking Amy and me under your collective wings and for nurturing her like a newborn chick — I thank you. My editors, Gill Evans and Annalie Grainger, deserve a particularly huge thank-you. Especially Annalie, who is so *au fait* with Amy and Clover's shenanigans that at this stage she should really be writing book four! She licked this book into shape in record time, and I am truly grateful for all her careful attention.

To the lovely Jo Hump-D, for all the clever marketing and tour-type thingys; Alice and Eve in publicity, for flying the Amy flag at every opportunity; Katie, for the glowing cover; Jill and her team, for all the work on the YouTube trailer; and, of course, thanks to the wonderful Jane Harris and all the sales and marketing team, especially those who worked on the U.K. tour in February. And not forgetting Sean, Julia, Ruth, Hanna, Heidi, Jess, and finally Mr. Walker Books in Ireland, the *über*fab Conor Hackett! And thanks also to all the lovely folk at Candlewick, my U.S. publishers, especially Liz.

Kate Gordon is my special teen editor, fellow Gleek, and general genius-type person, and I'd be lost without her help. And she's coming to do work experience for me soon — how lucky am I? My own book-loving galley slave. And another special "Hi" to the lovely Michelle in Navan, for sharing her story with me.

I've had such a fun-packed year with tours, festivals, and school events, and I have to thank the team of people who have made all this possible. To Tom at Children's Books

Ireland, for all his Trojan work on the Wildest Dreams Tour — you're fab, darling! And to Mags and Jenny, for being amazing too. To Joy Court at Coventry, for organizing a fantastic event and being so kind, and to Anna and all the gang who run the Writers in Schools Scheme in Dublin.

Now I must mention the children's booksellers who get the books to you, the readers. I was one myself for many years, and I know just how important and cool (obviously!) they all are. So: much love to the amazing David O'Callaghan, a veritable Ulysses of a children's book champion; all the gang at Dubray, for their support, especially Ruth, Kim, and Mary Esther; Mary Bridget at Hodges; and Grainne at Hughes and Hughes, Dundrum, for the Girl Guide readers' badge meeting, complete with shark songs.

And, finally, a thanks to you, the lovely reader, who picked up this book in the first place, and who frankly must be a bit mad to be also reading this rather long and rambling thank-you letter. For the e-mails, letters, cards, and photos — I thank you from the bottom of my heart. Writing is a lonely old job, and hearing from YOU makes it all worthwhile!

My e-mail is sarah@askamygreen.com and do drop me a line or check me out on Facebook — sarahwebbwriter. I genuinely love hearing from Amy Greensters.

À *bientôt,**
Sarah XXX

* "Later, alligator" in "ze froggy language," as Amy calls it.